Praise for Dee Tenorio's *Test Me!*

"Don't let this story pass you by. Ms. Tenorio creates some delish characters and these are two of her best."

~ *Nickie Langdon, Romance Junkies*

"A tempting, yet emotional tale, TEST ME is a book I highly recommend."

~ *Jennifer Bishop, RRTErotic Reviews*

Rating: A+ "This was my first book by Dee Tenorio, but after reading it, it wasn't my last."

~ *Melisa, Simply Romance Reviews*

Look for these titles by

Dee Tenorio

Now Available:

Betting Hearts

Kiss Me Again

Midnight Trilogy series

Midnight Sonata

Midnight Temptation

Midnight Legacy

Test Me!

Dee Tenorio

A Samhain Publishing, Ltd. publication.

Samhain Publishing, Ltd.
577 Mulberry Street, Suite 1520
Macon, GA 31201
www.samhainpublishing.com

Test Me!

Print ISBN: 978-1-59998-965-5
Digital ISBN: 1-59998-699-X

Editing by Angela James
Cover by Scott Carpenter

First Samhain Publishing, Ltd. electronic publication: November 2007
First Samhain Publishing, Ltd. print publication: September 2008

Dedication

For my husband— Because best friends and great loves don't always come in one package and I'm so glad I find both in you.

Chapter One

What's your favorite sexual position?

Dr. Travis Carmichael stared at the clipboard burning a hole in his hand. He blinked. She had to be kidding.

How frequently do you have sex?

How frequently can you sustain complete erection per session?

What?

He stomped to the front desk, past the long and motley line of men, shoving aside a kid with more acne on his face than hair on his head. He extended the questionnaire. "What the hell is this?"

"A clipboard." Aside from the blasé answer, Jade—the heavyset black woman who ran the lab and everyone in it with laser precision—barely acknowledged his presence. Considering she usually chortled around him or offered him pastries, he knew she was screwing with him.

Frowning, he pointed out the unnerving papers. "I meant these questions."

"If you know what they are, why you asking me?"

"I'm not here as part of Vetta's study and you know it. I want to talk to her."

"Suuuure you do." She dragged out the "sure" to epic proportions while she accepted clipboards from the line that had moved around him, Acne Boy included.

"Jade." Probably not a smart move to sound like he was giving her a warning, but this was insane. *I'm a scientist, for shit's sake, not a subject.*

Jade stood, crossing her large arms over her, frankly, enormous breasts. She wore a violet and blue island-print tent dress of some sort with a matching swath about her head. Heavy braids streamed down her back and over her shoulders. An implacable expression—one he was unfortunately well acquainted with—graced her smooth chocolate face. "You wanna to talk to Vetta, you fill out the forms. *Next!*"

He didn't have time for this. He had his own project to tend to. Sort of. Unfortunately, he also had a line of men blocking his door and disturbing his work with their noise. But the woman before him was less likely to listen to him than all those men. Jade listened to no one.

He went back to his seat in a huff. Fine, he'd fill out Vetta's intrusive sex quiz if he had to. He just wouldn't do it the way she wanted.

With a smile, he began. He had a pretty good drawing hand. Little more than stick figures, really, but he had a knack for catching something defining in a person's character and incorporating it. Since there was a lot of room for description, Travis got expansive with his illustration. He took time with the details, making sure that anyone could tell the faces were his and Vetta's.

The rest of the questions he filled out with as much sarcasm as he could muster. By the second page, where there was room for a couple more lewd pictures, Travis decided his colleague had utterly lost her mind. She was obviously studying male sexual habits—maybe dating habits, if the relationship questions were any indicator—although he couldn't guess why. Vetta St. Claire didn't like to be around people, much less men. He should know, he was the person she liked to be around the least.

But after a few years living next door to her, he wasn't surprised. He'd deduced that this kind of worthless fluff was what the rich, bored and brilliant did with their time. Absolutely nothing worthwhile. He might be broke, but at least he was doing something with merit. Well, he *had* been anyway.

Finishing the sheet with a flourish, he stalked back to the front desk where Jade was still busy handing similar clipboards to the long line of eager men. She sighed, reaching out to snatch it from him. He watched her write a code at the upper right-hand corner. She stopped writing to stare at the drawing, then turned a raised eyebrow at him.

Travis winked.

"Hope you got to do some of this stuff already, Doctor-Man," Jade murmured as she flipped the page to look for more. "'cause once Vetta sees this, you *never* gonna do it again."

"Tell me about it," he grumbled. Vetta St. Claire could suck the sex drive out of a nymphomaniac. And not in the lesbian-*chic* way he occasionally imagined. "But she's got a line of people to beat before she gets me by the balls."

"Oh?" Sudden interest made her voice lilt while her amber eyes glowed, eager for some good gossip no doubt.

Back to the usual Jade in a heartbeat; happened every time. On the few occasions he'd riled her, as soon as she was interested in something else, her temper evaporated. He had to stifle the urge to stay frustrated. It wouldn't serve any purpose. Jade had moved on. Staying mad would only cost him energy. Hadn't he seen Vetta in various shades of purple doing just that?

"Who's her competition for you this month? A redhead maybe? Or did you find another blonde? You *know* she hates it when you date blondes."

He shook his head, wishing a new bed partner were the most important worry he had. "Only if my loan officers are getting prettier. Truth is, you two might finally have me out of your hair once and for all."

She frowned suddenly, creating a deep crease between her brows. "You going somewhere?"

He shrugged, leaning on the counter and feeling very resigned all of a sudden. "Most likely. No more fun and games watching us fight anymore though, pretty sure about that. My funding's run out and no one's real interested in picking up the mantle of my affection, if you know what I mean." He smiled at her as if it didn't matter.

Her warm golden gaze coursed over him with a maternal worry he thought she only reserved for Vetta. "She's upstairs." She pointed to a door he knew would lead to a stairway. It was the same in his half of the facility.

Before he could follow her instructions, she caught his arm, those worried eyes now glowing in a strange way; a sly way. "Don't worry, I'm sure something will come up. It always has before. I'm real good about sensing these kinda things."

"Sensing?" Jade was no psychic. She didn't have to be, she usually had everyone and everything arranged exactly the way she liked. "Don't go getting any ideas—"

"I would *never*."

As if he believed that. "I mean it, Jade. I don't need any help. I get along just fine on my own."

"Of course you do, sweetheart. Right on up those stairs,

you're getting in my way."

"As long as we're clear." They weren't any such thing and he knew it. Jade did what she wanted. But it wasn't like there was anything she could do about his grants, so what did he have to worry about?

Probably everything.

He nodded at her, tapped the countertop a few times with a nervous finger and went off to find Vetta, a sinking feeling in his gut that the best part of the afternoon had passed.

He started toward the stairway door, acknowledging a sense of nostalgia about the woman he was approaching. After years in school with Vetta St. Claire, a smart man would never have tempted fate by renting lab space with an adjoining two-bedroom apartment from such a creatively evil nemesis. But Travis was a poor man and they, by definition, didn't have the luxury of being smart when there was dirt-cheap lab space to be had. Yet, no matter how vehemently they argued and schemed, he didn't regret a single day he'd been here. Good days or bad, Vetta kept things interesting.

For two years, they'd shared this monstrous modern-day castle of a building. It was stone, cold and huge, consisting of two labs separated by a hallway they often used to echo their arguments. In all that time, he'd never been in her apartment. For all he knew he was headed into the Black Hole of Calcutta. He seriously doubted the place would have any personality or warmth. God knew Vetta was devoid of both. It would probably be more like a morgue.

Better yet, a crypt. Would he find her in a cobweb-covered casket? Probably not. Knowing Vetta, she'd be sleeping in a satin-lined, hermetically sealed, top-of-the-line casket with some prissy filigree on its glossy surface. It would have to be extra wide, too, because for some reason—winter or summer—

she was never wearing less than two oversize, high-end labeled sweatshirts that could take the shape out of Jessica Rabbit if they had to. Add on the lab coat and the woman was often a big white cloud of displeasure with a whipping wheat-colored braid for a scorpion tail. But that was typical Vetta, spending top dollar on things she didn't need to do or study, just because she could. He rolled his eyes, climbing the steps absently.

If he had her resources—her money, her mind, hell, even her high-society parents—the things he could do. More important, what he *would* do. But no, not Vetta. She felt safer running the world by funding the important research instead of conquering it herself. She could probably cure hunger if she put that oversize brain of hers to it, but she had yet to even try. He was sure she had valid reasons—valid to *her*, anyway—for the way she avoided doing any significant work, but he sure as hell never figured them out.

It wasn't like he hadn't tried, either. From time to time, he'd stay up late trying to crack the puzzle of Vetta St. Claire. Her father, the infamously known Penny St. Claire, owned a pharmaceutical company, mostly in the way that a dog owned fleas. He walked around with more money than any single human in the world ought to have and did pretty much whatever crossed his mind at any given time. Thankfully, not much seemed to cross Penny's mind at any one time.

Her mother was no help. Svetlana Swinton was a bizarre mishmash of hot Swedish sex fantasy/actress and goofball airhead. Travis tried not to think about her wacky maternal instincts, but it was impossible to think of the habitual divorcee without remembering them. The birthday parties she forced Vetta to accept, complete with childlike balloons and giant sheet cakes Vetta would later donate to whomever she could foist them on. Usually him. She might be absentee, but Svetlana could always be counted on to take her daughter to task for even the smallest infraction of good manners. Then there were her delusions that Vetta was a nice person. She still insisted on calling her malignant daughter "*Solstråle*"—Swedish for "sunbeam"—no matter how many looks of disbelief she received.

The ray of golden sun herself, however, could be steely-eyed, had the nerve of a rottweiler, and just as sharp of a bite. He couldn't begin to fathom how she'd managed to develop a two-hundred-point IQ and absolutely no ambition whatsoever.

Still, for all her annoying lack of substance, she made him work harder than he ever would have otherwise and made him laugh when he was damn sure she'd never hear. If things kept going the way they had been for him, he wouldn't even have that going for him. A man knew he was down on his luck when he considered tangling with Vetta St. Claire something to look forward to.

He was still pondering that depressing little speculation when he reached the top of the stairs. Belatedly, he searched for a door handle, even a door on which to knock, but neither existed and he was standing uninvited in her coffinless living room.

Then again, if there *had* been a door he would've missed the sight of his life. Vetta St. Claire, crossing the living room in front of him.

Naked.

Well, not naked.

She did have a towel on her head.

She must not have seen him because she bent down to a large vanity directly across from him and opened a bottom drawer.

Travis couldn't have looked away if his life depended on it. It wasn't just her ass that had his dick lifting its head—though it surely would have been enough. Firm cheeks curved wide enough for his hands to cover, probably to grip and lift, but not much more than that. Golden skin, still dripping here and there, made his mouth water, but that wasn't what strangled any sound of warning he could have uttered. Those sweet arches of her hips arrowed down to the keyhole shape between her thighs, granting him a shot of what looked like the sweetest pussy he'd ever seen.

A peach. Even from the ten-foot distance, he could tell she was shaved clean as a whistle. Full, plump labia glistening with more than water, if he didn't miss his guess. As she bent, the folds of her flesh opened a little more, revealing stark pink secrets and the swollen bulb of her clit.

Someone either had a waterproof vibrator or a hell of a showerhead.

How hard would it be to cross the room, drop to his knees and taste some of that honey? Not even a little. His dick swelled further, sensing conquest now, and his legs were in the mood to follow through with the fantasy. He could lick her, curl his tongue through her folds before delving deep into the honeypot. Or he could go straight for the gold and suck that fat little clit whole, making her come twice before she knew what hit her. If he was a real bastard, he'd skip the prelims completely, whip out his cock and pound the shit out of her until they both fell down, coming.

Instead, he coughed.

She spun on a gasp, just like he expected her to, her towel losing its grip as she grabbed the edges of her armoire in shock. It was a new look on Vetta. But then again, so was nudity. If he'd thought looking at her ass had him going, it was like getting hit by a train to see her from the front. He let his eyes devour the shape of her breasts—full, pouting and round at the bottom where they'd fit in a man's hand—the nip of her trim waist, the gentle flare of her hips. Just as he'd thought—hoped?—she didn't have a hair on her. No trimmed muff for those long fingers of hers to get chafed on.

My favorite.

She stared at him, her unusual grey-green eyes wide, speechless. That might be his favorite too, since all they ever managed to do was fight. For the first time outside his obscure fantasies, her mouth was open and waiting for him in a perfectly shaped "O".

Since she had no audible objections, Travis felt free to take in the rest of her. To think, for seven years he'd known this woman, spoken to her on a near-daily basis and never had any idea she had a perfect pair of legs. Slim, long and strong, he could just imagine how they'd feel hooked over his hips, pulling him in just a little deeper on the down thrust. Maybe her knees bent over his forearms so her thighs were nice and wide would be better. He suddenly pictured those finely boned ankles over his shoulders and damn near gave himself a stroke.

"Travis." There wasn't any inflection in her tone but it broke through his thought processes before he gave his favorite jeans an ignominious stain.

"Travis!" she repeated, waking up enough to yank the towel that was slipping off her head, revealing the wet, tawny strands of her long hair. She hurried to cover herself, but it wouldn't matter. No amount of layered clothing was going to blind him to that body again.

Finally seeing a blush rise from her heart to her cheeks, he dutifully turned in place, bringing a hand up to cover his eyes so she'd have nothing to complain about.

"How dare you?" she raged behind him anyway, her movements sharp enough to make the air between them crack as she shook out her towel.

He turned back to her with a shrug. “You don’t have a door, Vetts. Anyone could have walked in. You’ve got a couple hundred men down there, answering questions about how they like sex to run. Didn’t it occur to you one or two of them might like to watch?”

Her left eye narrowed, nearly ticking at him. “It didn’t occur to me that *you* were a voyeur.”

He smiled. “I didn’t know either. But hell, you give a show like that and there isn’t a man in his right mind that isn’t going to look. Unless he’s gay.”

Her eyes flickered down to his prick, then back to his face. No doubt about it, there was a touch of surprise to the purse of her lips...not to mention a bit of concern. Her cheeks reddened further when she met his questioning gaze and he figured out what the concern was about.

Definitely a showerhead girl.

“I’m not gonna jump you, Vetta.”

“You’d be stupid to try.” She lifted her chin and tightened her hold on the top of her towel. If he didn’t know her better, he’d think she almost looked disappointed.

“I don’t need to jump you. From what I could tell, you’re already more than satisfied for the day.”

“How did you—” She bit her lip to keep herself from talking but the admission was out. She blanched, her eyes widening in horror.

Travis tucked his hands into his jeans pockets and rolled back on his heels. He kept his need to smile to himself. She’d probably kill him if she found out he was imagining that mole on the underside of her left breast.

The silence stretched out. She was holding onto her

indignity with both hands but Travis refused to be sorry. If she didn't want people to know she masturbated, she should get her clothes on before she came out of the bathroom.

Finally, she gave up with a huff. "I trust you have important issues to discuss, Doctor, but do you think this might wait until I'm dressed?"

"Don't go to any trouble for me, honey." It took his all not to laugh at the pinched expression on her face at that one. She could yell until she was blue in the face from now on and he'd never be able to take it seriously again. He'd just picture that mole and all her insults would roll right off him. "I need the zoo you've got out there to settle down. They're blocking my door."

"Fine." Just like that. One word, nothing like the usual argument any request from him entailed.

Never one to look a gift horse in the mouth, he nodded and started back down the stairs.

Vetta scowled at her reflection in the still-steamy mirror of her bathroom. *How did he know?*

She actually hadn't finished with her shower, having only done the basic rinsing before allowing herself a tension-reliving orgasm. Old hand took on new meaning as she came quickly and effectively. The sense of dissatisfaction afterward led her to leave the shower stall in a quest for a toy she'd ordered a few months ago when yet another bout of insomnia had her surfing online for anything of interest. The package was stuffed in the bottom cabinet of the armoire Jade used for a buffet table in the living room. Over the years, Vetta had discovered that the best way to hide anything from her curious friend was to hide it in practically plain sight. Not that Jade would have figured this one out if she found it anyway. A funny little pink ergonomic thing shaped, oddly enough, like a smooth tongue, the ad had promised sensual pleasure she'd never be able to imagine. She doubted they could conceive her imagination, but it was worth a shot.

When it arrived in a lovely plain box that didn't invite Jade to investigate its contents, she deemed the small tongue an excellent and effective purchase without even trying it out. But one small cough, one look in Travis's whiskey-colored eyes and she nearly came while the thing was still deactivated in her hand. She looked at it now, shook her head and left it on the counter before stepping back into the stall, her desire for any of its twenty-three speeds dissipated.

Instead, confusion stirred her senses. Travis Carmichael was sexy, that much could never be debated. She'd be lying if she claimed he hadn't starred in a few of her involuntary, strangely satisfying fantasies. What always bothered her about Travis was that she liked him. Almost as much as she couldn't stand him. Tall, rangy, wide-muscled men with shaggy blond hair and devil-may-care attitudes never really did it for her. But those qualities worked for Travis. He'd paid his way through college as an athlete, something that set him apart from all the other men in her post-graduate classes, and her body refused to be unimpressed.

And now the man apart had seen her naked.

And knew she'd fingered herself scant minutes before he walked in.

She leaned against the tiled wall, telling herself that what he thought didn't matter. His seeing her naked didn't mean anything. Travis had seen countless women naked, she wasn't going to stand out. But the look in his eyes... Her legs began to tremble and she could feel herself getting wet at just the memory. His gaze felt like fire.

She closed her eyes, letting herself sink deeper into the

sensation of those eyes memorizing her shapes and contours. For endless seconds, she'd basked in that approval. Tingled and responded to it, exactly as she responded to it now. The warm water turned her skin slick, making it easy for her practiced fingers to follow the current to the wetter folds between her legs. She sighed, both relieved and tormented, her clit throbbing as the side of her finger grazed it. This was no time for a slow build. She needed release. She moved her other hand to glide over her breasts, lifting and dragging across her now-sensitive nipples. How would his shadowy stubble feel on her skin as he took one tip, then the other, into his mouth? Would the abrading leave her tender...or begging for more?

She concentrated on remembering every aspect of Travis's gaze; dark and hungry, powerful and restrained. He wanted her. If he hadn't held himself back, he could be in that shower stall with her. Her body trembled harder, straining now for the fantasy to become more real. What if it were *his* hand gently teasing her nipples? What if it were his hand finding the hard long shape of her clit and fitting his fingers on either side to flick it carefully?

She moaned. Her nerve endings felt like they were electrified. She wanted to cup a hand over her own mouth, but she didn't want to take it off herself. Didn't want to take anything away from the illusion. She closed her eyes tighter and Travis materialized in her mind's eye, his careless smile tripping her heartbeat. With a sigh, she dipped deeper into the fantasy.

His *mouth* closed over her clit, the wetness from his tongue lapping at her instead of the shower flow. He licked the rounded flesh, the tip of his tongue making the tiniest flutter beneath the small head. Yes, then he began a rhythm of sucking and licking that had her laying her back against the tiles of the shower, nearly forgetting to breathe.

The whole of her pussy vibrated and throbbed. She was

barely moving her hand now, picturing him kneeling before her, hands on her thighs, pushing them apart far enough to smile wickedly before dipping his tongue into her...

She jerked at the crushing wave of her orgasm, gasping loud enough to echo as she held onto the mental projection. His tongue, not her fingers, was moving the heavy juice across her clit. Yes, his tongue, gliding deep into her, pumping until she could do nothing but shiver and shake, the fucking of his mouth rocking her to come so hard she cried his name as she slid slowly down the tiles to crouch in the water spraying on her from above.

Reality took its sweet time returning.

When it did, she leaned there, panting, every inch of her blissfully alive. By then, conscious thought returned as well. She wasn't surprised she'd suddenly found the key to better orgasms.

The problem would be not having them every time she felt Travis looking at her.

Chapter Two

Vetta made it a point to get dressed and come down to the lab, assuring herself that Travis wouldn't dare make two trips to her area in a single day. Still, she was sure to don an extra sweater, just in case. No matter what had happened upstairs—and after an hour of self-hypnosis, she'd all but convinced herself nothing had—she still had work to do. Mentally rubbing her hands together, Vetta anticipated getting into her latest research experiment: Had men, as a species, changed their motivating drive?

The question had niggled into her mind last year after yet another failed dating attempt. She met that particular bad fish at an alumni luncheon she'd been obliged to attend in her father's place. Carl Jeemers, thirty-year-old professor of genetics and lord of boredom. Poor Carl unwittingly helped her come up with something more interesting to think about than him—not that it was much of a challenge—the night he asked her to pay off his graduate studies. What were modern men truly motivated by?

It was still taught, of course, that man was driven by sex. That the natural inclination to spread his seed across the face of the planet was what gave him his dominating edge over every other species. But this was hardly the age of the caveman, when mastering use of his opposable thumbs designated him worthy to take over the world. Nowadays, man was another creature entirely, something the scientific community seemed blind to. In the twenty-first century, man was driven by something far more alluring than mere sex.

Money.

Vetta did consider that maybe men wanted money so they could *buy* sex, but after exposure to a few corporate raiders in pursuit of one of her father's pharmaceutical companies—not to mention the number of ever-present morons convinced they could offer sex for *her* money—she put that prospect to rest. Men wanted money for money. Period.

After that, all she had to do was find a way to prove her theory.

Easier said than done.

She admitted to a few mistakes, a couple wrong turns, but she was pretty sure she had it right this time. Despite something niggling at the back of her mind, she had gone over and over her hypothesis and not found a flaw. There wasn't a loophole left unsewn or a possibility unconsidered, so she dismissed the doubt as nonproductive. This experiment would run and if there was anything she missed, she'd find it in the data. For now, she could only move forward with the pieces she had.

The first step was to find a study subject; a perfect specimen, as it were. She researched via interview what women wanted in a perfect man. Intelligence ranked high, virility, experience and a sense of humor followed quickly after. They also wanted a man who was well traveled, who could listen to them and understand what they needed.

The next step, after this paragon of heterosexual manliness was found, was to see if he would sign a contract to give up women for the period of one year. That meant no relationships with a woman other than his immediate family or sex of any kind. He would make weekly semen deposits, which would be monitored for consistent sperm count as well as keep a diary of any and all sexual stimulants and nocturnal emissions. His reward would be a monthly stipend. At year's end, he'd have made a million dollars and Vetta, albeit only in a test-experiment phase, would have made her point: Men would *gladly* sacrifice sex for money—even the so-called good ones.

Now, it was true, most people would at least *try* to give up sex for money, especially a lot of money. She'd had to take that into account, but the extended amount of time required and the sheer invasiveness of the study would be more than enough to scare off all but the most greedy. Failure to finish the study was already written into the contract. The miserable specimen would be required to refund all costs for the experiment thus far into his year, proving he was an idiot to pass up his opportunity. Completion of the study, however, would prove mankind's stunted evolution. Foolproof.

She couldn't wait.

Excited, Vetta started to look through the small stack of already processed applications that were on her desk.

Specimen 225—should he be telling the truth—was virile indeed. He had sex regularly, although he wasn't very discriminating. Unfortunately, he didn't travel and only had a mid-range paying job without any pressing ambition to better himself.

She decided to let the program weed him out and moved on to the next one. 226 wasn't much better. Lower IQ, higher age, although 226's virginity was a nice note. Sad for him, sad for the experiment, but a glimmer of hope for the species. Smiling, Vetta reached for the next application.

The moment she looked down at it, her breath caught in

her throat, making her choke until her eyes watered. When she could finally breathe, it was all she could do not to scream. There, on the page, were stick figures of Travis and herself. Having sex. Not regular sex, either. No, these were drawings of monkey sex, hanging-from-the-ceiling sex. God, the third page had one upside down! And in each and every one, there was a grinning Travis. Winking. She crumpled the sheets in her fist, standing up and sending her chair shooting back behind her.

Travis.

She looked up at the ceiling. It was night outside already, so she knew he was on the roof, toying with her telescope thinking she hadn't noticed his nightly excursions. She should have brought it inside when she saw him secreting up the utility stairwell last month, but no, she'd tried to be *generous*. After all, Travis was only trying to stretch his tiny little brain. Just went to show, no good deed went unpunished.

She eyed the papers in her hand.

No bad one would, either.

Mind made up, she pushed past the last of the day's potential subjects to the outer hall. She stomped up the steps, already imagining the sheer joy of shoving him right off her building. She pictured his brown eyes wide with terror as she wrapped her hands around his neck. Juvenile, probably, but satisfying. First he walked into her apartment uninvited, then he stared at her naked like he had the right and now he'd committed the ultimate crime.

He'd messed with her experiment.

This called for more than petty violence. Vetta paused at the door to the utility stairs in the hall between the labs and reminded herself that her mind was her greatest strength, especially where Travis was concerned. The man could turn everything else to his own advantage. She had to think this through. What could she possibly do to him that would be equivalent to toying with her projects?

Punishments materialized, but the mind she was counting on kept rendering him naked in her imagination. Winking. She rubbed at her eyes. The important part was to make him regret what he'd done but first, she'd have to get close to him. Travis knew her too well to let her within arm's reach. She'd threatened to choke him to death often enough. No, she'd have to come up with a reason for him to come to her.

Short of stripping down and throwing a tube of KY at him, she couldn't think of anything to lure him close.

New angle. What lured Travis to any woman? This one she had the answer to. After seven years of seeing his various flings come and go, she knew his type better than the periodic table. Silicone. Big hair. Visible thongs. Single-digit IQ. None of which were in her personal arsenal. He *did* have that whole white-knight-to-the-rescue thing when it came to women. Most of the ones he dated needed rescue of some sort, be it from their lives, their minds or their implants. It always seemed an utter waste of his intellect to deal with women who couldn't count to five but far be it from her to judge. Much. For once, however, his ingrained flaw could be used for her own ends. All she needed was a sob story and when he was close enough...she'd get him.

She rushed up the stairs, slamming through the door at the top, grinning at the satisfying boom of the metal door closing behind her. Oh, she was going to get him good.

Travis heard the slam of the roof door and groaned before stepping away from Vetta's prized telescope. He didn't know much about astronomy. He especially didn't know much about quality telescopes, but he knew he liked looking at the stars and Vetta's shiny white toy gave him an excellent opportunity.

He'd cheated a little and skipped the part about asking permission, so he also knew the slam of the door signaled oncoming doom. Especially since he'd kept the door open with a rock. Vetta being the only one with a key, he was going to be up here getting told off for as long as she wanted him to be. He mentally tallied the future argument to her. Not because she was right, but because she had him cornered.

By his count, he was up 22-15 this month. *22-16*, now. Too bad January couldn't go on forever. No doubt next month he'd get hammered again. She always did better on the shorter months.

Travis turned around, sinking his hands into his loose-fitting jeans, expecting to see Vetta storming her way over to him. Any time now, she'd be the avenging angel of expensive leisure equipment, yelling at him for messing with her instruments and accusing him of trying to rig it to break the next time she used it when they both would know she was really yelling at him for getting a good look at her kidneys.

Actually, rigging the scope wasn't such a bad idea, but not something he was in the mood for right now.

What he *was* in the mood for—a good hard fuck—wasn't going to happen either, so he was up shit creek no matter which way he paddled.

All day long, he'd been thinking about Vetta. Wondering what it would have been like if he'd just followed his impulse and taken a taste of that peachy puss. Would she have let him? Could he even now be balls deep inside her, feeling the solid slap of his hips colliding with her thighs, if only he'd given it a shot? It was a hell of a thing to have to second-guess. God knew his dick was tired of thinking about it. The damn thing hadn't given up hope, meaning he'd had a semi-erection off and on for hours.

Absolutely nothing got done.

How could it when he was too aroused to sit comfortably and too distracted to think? Making slides made him wonder if her golden skin was as sleek as it looked. Monitoring the growth of his tissue samples made him wonder how she'd managed to hide such a perfect set of breasts all these years without him figuring it out. Worse, every period he wrote was the exact size and shape of the mole on the underside of said perfect left breast. If he was stupid enough to stop working, he found himself wondering about Vetta and her trusty showerhead. What did she look like when she came? Was she the kind that got flushed from her nipples to her hairline? Did she moan or bite those full lips to keep the noise inside?

Dammit, now he had a hard-on again. Twenty-eight degrees outside and here he was, stiff as a fucking rebar.

If only she'd show up and remind him why getting her under him was such a shitty idea.

He scrubbed a hand through his hair, looking toward the shed-like roof entrance. It stood in the middle of the roof and he was conveniently on the backside of it. Still no sign of her. He fit the custom-made tarpaulin over the tripod and scope. Maybe he *wouldn't* lose this argument. He could simply tell Vetta he was just up here getting some fresh...er, frozen air. If that didn't work, fuck it, he'd just distract her with his woody. She'd run her frigid ass downstairs at light speed.

The sound of something odd drifted to him on the brisk breeze. It almost sounded like a choke. He frowned. Maybe a sob. Whatever it was, it wasn't good.

Carefully making his way toward the shed, he heard it again, this time louder. It was a woman, he could tell from the voice quality, but that was all he could deduce. Making sure his tennis shoes didn't make too much noise on the graveled surface of the roof, Travis moved to the other side of the small building.

When he circled it, he heard what was now a full-fledged crying jag, complete with odd snortling sounds. He stepped around the corner and blinked at the sight.

Vetta?

She was slumped against the gunmetal gray door, still regretfully closed, hands on her face and knees drawn up to her chest while she heaved and wailed. At least, he hoped those were her knees. She had on some kind of fleece skirt that had enough fabric to have required its own sheep farm.

He allowed himself a moment's cowardice to consider stepping silently back into the shadows to wait until her emotional outburst was over and she'd gone back inside.

Two things stopped him.

One, he couldn't leave a woman falling apart like this and not attempt to help her, even if it *was* Vetta. Two, if she left, she wouldn't prop open the door and he'd be stuck out here all night. He didn't allow himself to analyze which one was most important.

Instead, he crouched down next to her and placed one hand awkwardly on the back of her head. She stilled instantly under his touch, her body tightening in a way that even her voluminous folds of clothing couldn't hide. Then she looked up, her eyes dry, an unholy smile on her face as she reached out and shoved him back on his ass.

Maybe staying out here all night *wouldn't* have been so bad.

Casting a look over his shoulder, he gazed at the roof edge. Thirty feet wasn't such a far way to fall. He could survive. A broken femur and a couple fused vertebrae wouldn't be so hard to heal from, would they?

Looking back at Vetta, Travis had the sinking feeling he was about to find out.

"*You*," she growled.

"Me," he agreed, a lack of anything better coming to mind.

She scrambled to her usually impressive six feet and Travis was glad for his three inches over that. Height might be all he had on her, but at least it was something.

Well, it was when he was standing.

"You!" Definitely accusatory now.

He heard crumpling paper and saw she was clutching something in a death grip. The rolled sheets were just thick enough to be something he hoped it wasn't.

"You…jerk!" Vetta swatted the top of his head with the papers, making him yell out with the surprise of her attack.

She might say some awful things—things he had to go look up—but Vetta had never hit him.

The barrage of paper on his shoulders and head were increasing in tempo and strength. Over the shock, Travis set about getting away from her, rolling out of the strike zone and scrambling to his feet.

"What the hell are you doing?" He changed direction, moving back into the shadows. "I should have known it was a trap. *You?* With an emotional outburst? Nazis have less control than you do."

Vetta followed him, her lab coat iridescent in the night air. "You deserved it. I can't believe you drew pornography on a legitimate research application! Most of these things aren't even physically possible! And that *name! Harden Beefy?* You're the etiolated teratocarcinoma of the scientific community!"

Dammit, another one to Google. "Legitimate, my ass. That questionnaire read like a Penthouse Letter."

"As if you ever look at anything but the pictures!"

Good point, but he wasn't conceding or slowing his retreat. He needed every step he could get or Vetta would be giving him another lesson in the art of bushwhacking. It was time to try reasoning with her.

"It's not like I planned it. Jade wouldn't let me in to talk to you until I filled one out."

"Oh, *that's* a mature reason! It's not *my* fault, the big mean *woman* made me do it!"

"Vetta!"

"Don't you *Vetta* me, Travis Carmichael! After everything you've already done today, you had to go and think up something worse?"

"I did this first, actually—"

That probably wasn't the best way out of the situation because she nearly exploded with renewed energy and quickened her pace. Too bad he was running out of roof.

"It's not like I *knew* you were going to be naked when I went into your apartment. You were the one strolling around the place without a stitch."

"Oh, sure, blame *me* now. How dare I forget something before going into the shower?"

All right, enough of this bullshit. Travis caught her wrist with one hand, meeting her crackling gaze with one of his own. "We both know you'd already been in the shower, Vetta. Admit it, you're just mad because I knew what you were doing in there."

"Can't you keep your brain on the subject, you pervert?" she snarled, but he noticed she did nothing to yank her hand free.

He hitched a shoulder. "Hey, I'm only human. You don't

have to be a pervert to enjoy looking at a honeypot like yours."

She froze, wide eyes not even blinking for a solid three seconds. "H-honeypot?"

He liked the stunned look on her face. Stunned and *curious*. The wind was definitely out of her sails, but if the way her full lips parted meant anything, she didn't care about being mad. He pulled her a little closer, getting a hint of coconut in the air despite the cold gusts. He felt his cock twitch against the cushion of her skirt; the damn thing was happy. It'd be a hell of a lot happier if it was ramming up *into* said honeypot, but he wasn't stupid enough to expect that. Any second now, she'd come to her senses and slap the shit out of him. Then his raging libido could go back to pretending it didn't like her.

The sooner that happened, the better.

"You know what I'm talking about, Vetta," he murmured, watching her mouth the way he always did when she didn't know he was there. Tonight, it was soft, pink and slightly open. If the light were better, he'd see the moist color of her tongue. She might say the worst things, things to make a man check if his nuts were still in place, but she had lips that could put Viagra out of business in a day. And he would do or say anything to make himself forget it. Like piss her off. Royally. "You can say it. Pussy."

Her eyes flickered, probably from shock. She didn't use language like that. No one used it around her. The unspoken rule in dealing with Queen Elizabeth, reincarnate.

"I...I can't say that."

For the briefest of seconds, they stared at each other, surprised. Any other day, she'd have castrated him through his nostrils for talking to her that way.

Maybe he didn't know Vetta as well as he thought.

He smiled, his heartbeat kicking up while his dick swelled

to full staff. If she didn't bust him outright it could only be because she *wanted* to say it. And damn if he wouldn't love to hear her. Vetta, down and dirty. That could keep him hard for days.

"Sure you can, sweetheart. Put your lips together, like a kiss."

She gave her head the tiniest of shakes, reminding him of someone under a spell they couldn't break. "I...I can't."

He took another step, pressing her firmly against his body, making her feel him by wrapping his arms around her and pulling her into him. Even with the thick layers of clothing, she would feel him. "Put your lips together."

Maybe it was the lack of asking, but she managed it without a complaint.

"Say it slow, Vetts. Feel your way around it. Let your tongue play with it."

"Why are you doing this, Travis?" Suspicion overrode the desire on her face.

He decided to be honest. "Because your pussy is all I've been thinking about ever since I saw it." He leaned down, grazing her ear with his mouth, taking a deep pull of that coconut scent. "I want to know what it tastes like, Vetta."

She gasped, wrapping her hands around his biceps, trembling against the side of his face. But she didn't push him away.

Frowning, he realized she wasn't going to. If anything...she liked this. If he weren't so damn hard and ready to ride, he'd be laughing. Virginal Vetta was getting off on dirty talk. He let his hands get a grip on her ass, squeezing the cheeks hard in each hand, bowed his head closer to her ear when he felt the shudder of her breath on his neck.

"I was going to lick you when I saw you." He closed his eyes, remembering every shiny centimeter of her. "I was going to get right behind you and suck that fat little clitty of yours. I wanted my tongue inside you, Vetta. I wanted to fuck you until you came all over my face. And then you know what?"

He waited, wondering if he'd gone too far when the pause lasted nearly a minute. Until, faint, less than a whisper, she asked, "What?"

And she was his. Tonight. He knew it. Hell, his dick knew it. The only question was how to get enough clothes off to do it without getting hypothermia on the required equipment.

"I was going to pick you up and fuck you against your living room wall. Fuck you until you screamed."

"You can't do that."

"You planning on stopping me?" Here it comes. Total shutdown. Vetta's revenge. He waited, trying not to breathe raggedly.

"No, I mean I don't scream. I've never screamed."

How the hell did she manage to sound matter-of-fact about fucking against a wall?

"Get those vocal cords ready then."

"Wh—" was all she got out before he kissed her. Catching her mid-sentence meant her mouth was open, all the better for him. In no time, he was toying with her tongue, guiding her a step at a time toward the closed door of the roof shed. It wouldn't be warm, it wouldn't be gentle, but dammit, it was going to be good.

Her lab coat hit the ground first. They both walked all over it. Her hands were on either side of his face, pulling him along, her kisses untrained but definitely excited. He couldn't figure out how to get the sweaters off, so he dug his hand underneath them, following the silk of her skin to the unbound breasts. Hard little points stabbed his palm as he took hold. Vetta pulled away from the kiss, throwing her head back on a sigh. A good thing, too, because they'd reached the door. Rucking up the fabric, he gave himself a whole second to enjoy the sight of her bare breasted again. Then he dove down and pulled the first peachy tip into his mouth.

Her hands clawed his head, but he didn't care. He sucked her nipple in deep, keeping the other warm with his hand, working the tips for all he could. She squirmed, she sighed, but she didn't lie. Not so much as a peep escaped her. More drastic measures needed to be taken.

The heavy skirt she wore wasn't the easiest thing to pull up, but he managed it. He had to let the sweaters fall back into place, using both hands to sneak under the iron curtain and pull down what felt like the tiniest scrap of silk he'd ever felt. He didn't bother looking. Not when that golden pussy was right there, already wet and waiting to be sucked.

"Hold this for me, honey." He took her hands and wrapped them around the folds of her skirt. Then he put one hand on each trembling thigh and pushed them gently apart.

A minute ago, if you'd asked him, he would have said that he would dive right in if he ever got a chance to go down on Vetta St. Claire. But here, now, he realized he needed to be gentle. He needed to show care and build her slow.

Because if he wanted to make her come screaming—more important, if he wanted to do it more than once—he was going to have to do it right.

So, he reached a hand to graze over her warm skin, listening to her shuddering breath. His thumb slipped into the pouting main fold, finding the clit that had all but waved at him earlier. He didn't touch it. Instead he circled around it, letting her feel the texture of his skin. With his other hand, he cupped her, letting his fingertips gather the heavy juice that seeped from the source. She jumped when he let one finger in, deep enough only to tease, then pulled it out again.

Her legs widened, offering him the entire golden puss, but he had no interest in relieving the tension. He continued to play, ignoring the heavy throb of his cock, ignoring the cold or the sounds of traffic below. He parted her outer labia, letting the cool air dance through the hot folds inside. He held her that way, hovering his mouth over her for a full second before finally letting his tongue taste her sweetness.

Peaches would never be the same again.

All intentions disappeared. There was only the flavor, sweet, thick like honey, just the slightest tang of astringent. Enough to entice his taste buds toward deeper mysteries.

"Oh, my God," Vetta whispered, nearly sounding like a shout in his ears. But not a scream, not yet. Her knees nearly gave, so he shored her up by the hips, holding her exactly where he wanted her so his tongue could glide right up inside her. He wanted to lap at her, to suck her dry, but he wasn't able to exercise that kind of control. She was shaking, riding his tongue while his nose made friends with her clit. It took all his will to pull free, though he couldn't help circling that clit one more time before he let her go and began working on his belt buckle.

"Travis...Travis, please."

He shoved the denim down, shorts as well, freeing the thick rod and pumping it once or twice with his own hand before taking her. She'd been tight and this was a hell of a lot bigger than his tongue.

"Do you want to come now, Vetta?"

He licked her to make sure she was listening.

"Yes."

"Then you have to say it."

"Say what?"

He stood up, using his hand to guide the tip of his eager cock to her clit, rubbing them together so they made friends. She moaned. God, *he* moaned. No pussy had ever felt that good and he wasn't even inside this one yet.

"You know what I want you to say."

She opened her eyes, moving her hips forward over his stick, damn near ruining the whole teasing thing with one deft move. She grabbed a fistful of his sweatshirt. "No, damn you, I don't."

He couldn't help it, he laughed, leaning down to kiss her, giving her a taste of herself with a deep kiss. "Tell me where you want my cock, Vetta, and I'll give it to you."

She lifted her leg, pushing against him enough for shallow penetration, but it wasn't what she wanted. It wasn't enough. "Travis—"

He gave her a little more, then pulled back. "Say it, Vetts."

"My pussy!" she gasped, shuddering hard. "Put it in my pussy."

Which is exactly what he did. Hard. All the way, in one thrust, making her sob with relief and shock.

"Now's where we have fun." Grabbing her ass, he lifted her off the ground, leaving her no choice but to wrap those long limbs around him if she wanted to keep him inside. And she did want it. Just as bad as he did.

Taking hold of her hips, he pulled back, earning a whimper, then rammed up into place. Right where he belonged. She clutched his head, her elbows digging into his shoulders, but he didn't care. Heavy thrusts pushed a sound from her, while that incredible puss squeezed around him, grasping him over and over again.

"What am I doing to you, Vetta?"

"You're—"

"I'm fucking you. Say it."

"Ah—"

Long thrusts turned short and fast, the slap of their skin matching the metal on metal jangling of the door to its jamb. He could feel her tightening around him, making the pleasure sharpen so that his balls were rising, preparing to fill her. There wasn't much time left for either of them.

"What am I doing?" He wasn't in control anymore. His body was and it wasn't waiting for his petty little fetishes. Her hips rolled into his thrusts, urging him on, her breath coming in pants with faint little noises escaping at the end. He thrust faster, harder, willing her to take it and give him what he needed.

"You're fucking me, Travis," she finally said in a harsh whisper into his ear. "Fucking me...fucking...*fuck*—" It wasn't a scream, but it was enough. He ground into her, just as her knees clenched around his back and her pussy greedily throbbed around him, drinking every last drop he could offer. He laid his head on her shoulder while she gasped roughly against his neck.

She continued to pulse around him, leaving him just one thought.

What the hell were they going to do now?

Chapter Three

Disentangling from Travis wasn't nearly as hard as escaping him.

What had she done?

One second, she'd been yelling at him, ready and willing to berate him for his utter lack of respect. The next...well, she still wasn't sure what happened next. His eyes took on that angry, hungry gleam and he started saying things that got her head pounding from her heartbeat racing. All she'd been able to think about was the way he had made her feel in her shower, which made no sense analytically because he hadn't really been there in the first place.

After the sex—could you call it losing your virginity if you'd already tossed that on a vibrator?—she hadn't known what to do. She'd never planned on her first time with a man being outside, against a door, still dressed and with a man she couldn't stand. All she could think of was getting away.

She'd pushed at his shoulders, disconcerted at how comforting it felt to be cradled in his hold that way. She didn't want to be soothed by the silk of his hair against her cheek or the warmth of his breath. She didn't want to be held as if she was precious. She didn't even want his hands on her ass. She just wanted to be free.

"Vetta," he grunted when she pushed harder, setting one of her feet on the ground and forcing him to slip free from her body.

She pretended that the slippery sensation didn't make her shiver, that the sudden absence of him from inside her didn't make her feel empty. Her skirt fell back to her ankles, covering all evidence as to what had happened. To her, at least.

Travis backed up a step, his jeans still open, his penis still exposed, still wet...still nearly erect. He quickly went to work covering up, but when she dared to look in his eyes, she could see that an apology was forming. Or maybe it was just a reflection of the confusion inside herself.

His eyes were downcast and the stark lighting of the fluorescent lights on the roof made his expression hard to read. All she could see now were the wide planes of his cheekbones, the grim line of his mouth and the shadows in his eyes.

"I have to go," she blurted, spinning in place and frantically reaching for the flat handle of the doorknob. She yanked it down, but the door wouldn't open.

"Vetta, we need to talk about this."

"No, we don't." They would never talk about this. She had no inclinations whatsoever to be mocked. She was twenty-five years old. If she wanted to have meaningless sex on the roof of her own property, she would.

"Vetta." His voice was gentle. Gentle. From Travis!

"I've dropped into the twilight zone," she muttered, reaching for her keys from her lab coat pocket. Except she wasn't wearing her lab coat. Feeling wild now, she looked around, ignoring his attempts to get into her frame of view. Finally, she saw it, floating like a phosphorescent ghost a few feet away. She hurried over, snatching it from the ground and reaching into the pocket with growing desperation. The lump of keys, just where they usually were, jangled into her palm. She turned back to the shed door and found Travis waiting, arms crossed, decidedly in her way.

"Move."

He shook his head. "Not until we talk."

"What's to talk about? We had sex. We're done."

Against the door that way, his expression was even more inscrutable than before. She hoped he couldn't see any better than she could. Despite his flaws, the man was a brilliant observer. If he realized for one second her disconcertion, she'd never hear the end of it. What she needed was to go downstairs, take a shower and hide in her room until this entire situation faded into obscurity. She did not need to talk about it.

"Why are you running away?"

Was he stupid? "This was a mistake, Travis."

"Why do you say that?"

Yes, he was. He really, really was. "Because you hate me. Because I don't like you."

She watched him shrug. "You of all people should know sex doesn't have anything to do with liking one another. It's about chemistry. Need. Desire."

She balled her fingers around the keys, his words making a sick feeling in her stomach. She'd been the one to say it, but oddly, it hurt having him agree to hating her. Thankfully, she'd long ago learned how to keep from showing a response to things said or written about her. Growing up, her mother's stardom and her father's money had made her a target for the press. Nothing Travis could say would be worse than what any of them had said.

"You wanted me," he continued, proving her incorrect again. "There's nothing wrong with that."

"Will you *please* move away from the door?" Moisture was dripping down her leg and she preferred to be mortified in peace.

"I wanted you too, Vetta," he added quietly.

"Good," she snapped. "Great. We wanted. We got. Satisfied?"

"Not even close to it."

She wished she could reply, wished she had something to say that would shut him up, but opening her mouth yielded no sound at all.

Travis sidestepped the door, finally getting out of her way. He even waved her through, bowing gallantly, his dark stare never leaving her face. Refusing to be afraid—of what exactly, she didn't know—she made herself go back to the door, moving past him to unlock it with the keys.

As she searched for the right one, Travis slipped behind her. His body blocked the breeze, emitting a heat that had her skin tingling again. He leaned down to her ear, as if he were going to touch her, but made no contact. The correct key slid into the lock on the door.

"It's not over yet, Vetta."

She yanked down the lever. "Like hell it's not."

He lay his hand over hers, pulling the heavy door open. Voice deep, intimate, probably subconscious staining, he whispered, "You can't hide from things you don't want to face. Your problems will always be there when you turn back around."

Vetta stumbled, but he caught her elbow.

"I'm not saying this to scare you. I just know that we've started something here, whether we like it or not."

"Something stupid," she corrected as primly as she could.

He nodded his head. "Maybe. It's not good timing for either of us. You've got your weird little experiment and I have..."

She frowned at him when his voice trailed off, then shook her arm free. "I'm not going to be your convenient lay, Travis. This was a one-time thing because you saw me naked. We were curious. Don't make more of that than it was."

That seemed to snap him out of his little mini-trance. "I don't have to. Sooner or later, we're going to end up in bed. It's just a matter of time."

She tromped down the stairs, determined not to look back or listen. She made it all the way through her lab and to the stairs before being indignant couldn't carry her any farther. Her shaking knees dumped her on the bottom step. She dropped her head in her hands and sighed.

"Baby, is that you?" Jade called from the apartment above.

"Yes," she answered, her voice a little shaky, but hopefully not too much so.

"What are you doing down there? I've been calling for you for an hour. Your dinner's cold." She could hear Jade's voice coming closer to the threshold. "Come on up, I don't wannat to be yellin' all night."

"I'll be up in a second," she replied, feeling better about the strength in her voice. So what if she was wiping strange tears off her cheeks. It was idiotic to be disappointed. Until now, her sex life had consisted of her hands, plastic toys and a lot of erotic reading. An eager, thorough, sexy man, a mind-blowing orgasm and an outdoor adventure were things a girl could only dream of for her first time. But the whole thing with Travis was so...*sordid.*

It was one thing to think graphically when touching yourself. She still felt a little queasy about speaking the words he clearly enjoyed. About the way it made her feel—wet, quivery, even a little orgasmic—but more so about what it did to her to hear it coming from Travis. He'd never made any bones about being rough around the edges. It was part of his charm, when he chose to use any. A woman looked at him and figured he gave it hard and energetically. She felt a flush and a touch of a backflash, remembering the feel of his cock inside her, far wider and longer than anything she'd ever had the courage to purchase. Her thighs trembled again as she clenched them together to end the sensation. Or maybe to prolong it? She didn't know anymore.

She didn't *like* Travis. Didn't like the antsy way he made her feel or the way he constantly questioned her motivations. She wasn't evil, for pity's sake. She had parents who—together—had the impulse control of a two-year-old. Apart, they were even worse. She'd spent her life raising them, a task made more and more difficult by their divorce, her father's absent but happy existence and her mother's string of pointless marriages.

The two of them were always attracting press and paparazzi. Tack on Jade, the nanny they'd hired to keep up with her, who saw it as her life's work to get Vetta married off, and Vetta had her hands full. If that made her the tiniest bit controlling, oh well. If it made her *more* than a tiny bit lonely, she'd have to oh well that, too. It did *not* mean she had to get kinky.

Except, clearly, she liked being kinky.

She dropped her face into her hands wishing she could come up with a real reason to cry other than incredible sex. Then again, maybe she did have a right to shed a few tears. A girl should be able to hope and dream the first man she had sex with was someone meaningful. Someone who cared about her. God, at least someone who *liked* her. But she wouldn't cry for long. She wiped her face as best she could, walked up the stairs and smiled at Jade on her way to the shower. If Jade's eyes narrowed with suspicion...there was plenty of room left on the "oh well" list.

☙

Travis refused to feel guilty about splurging on some rolled tacos from the local Albertos. Three measly bucks was not going to save him and it was probably the last treat he was going to get for some time. He had enough guilt to deal with since walking down from the roof, not liking himself very much for the way he handled Vetta. He wasn't wrong about what he'd said—he had no doubts whatsoever they'd be denting her mattress or any other conveniently flat surface—but something was wrong with her that he couldn't put his finger on. He'd just have to find out from her later what it was. Until then, his overactive conscience would continue its field day.

After walking past the large group of men wrapping themselves around the building, he checked his mail in the oddly quiet foyer. When he stepped past the main doors into the hallway between the labs, he saw it. His last feasible chance at continuing his work lay in his hand and he already knew what the outcome would be.

The end had finally come. It was over.

He ripped the envelope from the Lissex Research Corporation open, but it was exactly what he expected; a last-ditch effort that hadn't worked. There was, of course, that million to one possibility of the Brassett Board of Medical Science decision due in a few weeks, but he was more likely to willingly get a sex change than get that grant.

No, at the end of the month, he'd officially be out of grant money. He'd also be homeless, broke and probably starving.

Goody.

He crumpled the sheet of paper in his hand. Lissex was an obscure non-profit organization that funded several anticancer studies. They were a long shot to begin with—though still not a leap of faith like the Brassett Board—but he thought the small award might sustain him until he could make other arrangements.

While we definitely feel your studies into the effects of true and synthesized estrogen on women of advancing age are fascinating in their own right, we do not have room in our budget for you...

How often had he read that in the last several months? So many he'd nearly lost count. Some were polite, some were blunt; all of them declined. Estrogen research was a hot study topic these days. So much so that only the most innovative angles won the awards. Not that he was after recognition. He was after a cure. Still, his dedication didn't make an impact on the people making the grant decisions. Everyone had a story, grant committees had no time to listen to them and none of those stories could matter.

But they mattered to Travis. *He* was the one who had promised a dying mother he would make a difference in finding a cure. *He* had watched that vibrant, independent woman in her prime be sapped of her strength, her confidence, her very life. He couldn't hate them for not knowing how important his research was to him. But he could hate them for not caring. Still, until today, he'd had hope.

Now he had nothing.

Nothing except broken promises, a weary soul and a great big lab that for all intents and purposes was now a glorified storage unit.

The rolled tacos in his hands lost their allure in an instant.

Feeling like he was dragging, he stepped into the hallway and wasn't the least bit surprised to find twenty guys in there—down by half—sitting in folding chairs pressed to the wall, quietly waiting for Jade to hand them clipboards to fill out. Vetta still had her strange little experiment to run, after all.

Jade stood in front of the men like a four-star general and every last male in there stared wide-eyed as chastised six-year-olds.

"You want in, you be quiet and stop arguin'. Everyone plays nice or no one gets a shot at that million. You got me?"

Travis felt his eyebrows rise along with the hair on the back of his neck. Million? As in *dollars*? What the hell was Vetta up to now? Seriously. If she were handing out money like that, his last few weeks in this building would be utterly without peace.

Continuing down the hall toward Jade, he got a shock and a half when the big woman, wearing eye-stinging fuschia this time, turned and blinded him further with a smile. Vetta obviously had not filled her in about the fuck up on the roof.

"Hey, Doctor-Man!" She looked down at the white paper bag in his hand and sniffed. "What's that?"

He looked down, shrugging. "Lunch?"

"It's fast food." He'd swear that was what she said, but is *sounded* like "it's hazardous waste".

"It's really very good." His assurance didn't take the sneer from her lip. "I'm sorry?"

"Good. I'll send you something better, soon as I finish. Here, make yourself useful."

His treat disappeared with a flash of her hand—or was that her dress?—replaced by a stack of clipboards and applications. "Um..."

"Over there. That side. The sooner they work these

through, the sooner the hall is clear."

Forget lunch, getting rid of the crowd was impetus enough. Travis clutched the pile of boards and started handing them out as fast as he could.

"So, what's this experiment about, anyway?" he asked, halfway down the row.

"Vetta didn't tell you last night on the roof?"

Travis froze.

"Oh yeah, I know about that." Jade's deep laughter had him turning to look over his shoulder at her. "Just hand those out. We'll talk after."

Why did that sound like a threat?

Twenty minutes later, Travis sat at one of his four long lab tables, Jade across from him watching him devour heaven on a spoon while she wiped her forehead with a handkerchief.

"What's this called again?" he asked between bites of the hearty stew.

"That's jambalaya, that's rice pilaf and that under the towel is fresh apple pie."

He felt his eyes bulge. "A whole one?"

"You think I cut 'em before I serve 'em?" She took a polite taste from her own serving.

He put his spoon down. "You did all this because I bought takeout?" He needed to catch Jade in the hallway more often.

"No, I did all this 'cause I like you and 'cause you so skinny I been looking for a way to fatten you up for years."

Travis smiled at her. Unlike her grown ward, Jade had no reason to lie about liking him or not. He picked up the utensil and dug back in. "Thanks. This is really great."

"Don't thank me yet, I still got plans for you."

"Pwanz?" he asked around his spoon, not liking the sound of that word.

She nodded, an unholy gleam in her light brown eyes. Twin dimples showed on either side of her face, sinking deep into her full, brown cheeks.

Travis swallowed, then choked for a full minute before having the courage to ask, "What kind of plans?"

"Oh, nothing you can't handle, Doctor-Man. Tell me," she said, leaning toward him across the table and making him wonder if he'd just sold his soul for a bowl of soup. "Have you seen the morning paper? Real interesting ads in there, if you can put two and two together."

He stared down at the circled text, mouth still full. Words burned themselves into his brain. *Offering one million to subject whose genetic material meets set requirements...* Vetta. This was her experiment? She was looking for genetic material? He glanced up at Jade, who shrugged. Then he remembered the night before, pumping himself into Vetta like a stupid kid, not thinking, not even caring about anything but getting deeper inside her and marking her while she whimpered around him. Suddenly, her little freak-out made sense. She hadn't been upset about the fuck. She'd been desperate to get herself cleaned up, terrified that she'd just gone and contaminated herself with an unworthy sperm sample.

His stool was loudly hitting the ground a good second or so after he grabbed the newspaper and stormed across the lab.

Chapter Four

Vetta spun around in her desk chair at the resounding boom of her lab door slamming shut nearly hard enough to shatter the glass on the upper half with none other than Travis Carmichael bellowing her name like a wounded moose.

She stood up, frowning since she'd *just* gotten the man out of her head, and began crossing from the back of the lab to the front. "Problem, Travis?"

Hands on his hips, he was huffing and puffing, looking like he didn't know where to start. That indicated several problems, all of them in full view of a few dozen applicants. Great.

While she waited for him to put a sentence together, she made the mistake of noticing his exposed forearms. Admittedly, it was because she wasn't feeling quite up to staring him in the eyes, but it was still a mistake. Travis in full lather was a sight that could get a woman's blood hot in 0.2 seconds flat on any regular day. The day after having rampaging sex with him? She didn't want to do the math on that one. Worse, he was wearing one of those super-soft, faded plaid shirts he lived in, sleeves rolled up, and her gaze coursed over the fine muscles moving while his hands flexed in anger. The not-so-slow burn began to churn inside her.

"We need to talk," he growled, his tone forcing her to glance up at him. He'd caught her ogling, probably knew how she was responding, but his dark eyes were snapping and not in pleasure.

She crossed her arms over her chest to get her bearings back. With any luck, it would slow down her heartbeat, too. "You sure you don't want to just paw the earth and snort?"

"Funny. Real cute, coming from you."

She couldn't see why, but knew better than to ask. Travis had a bad habit of explaining himself. She raised her eyebrow imperiously, the way she did when her father's financial advisors were trying to talk her into an investment she didn't like. As usual, she got the desired effect—incensed man-sputter.

"You're a real piece of work, you know that?" Travis barked, gesturing widely with his hands, his thick blond hair bouncing as he spoke. "I thought you took the cake when you started asking questions about sex practices, but this time you've ripped off the whole fucking bakery!"

"Do you intend to make sense in the near future, Dr. Carmichael? You're disturbing my staff." Not that Jade was anywhere in sight. Her two female assistants could have helped by looking something other than awed at the sight of a full-blown male snit.

"You're using this experiment for stud service!" Travis seethed, waving a newspaper at the sea of men. "Really, Vetta, paying a guy a million bucks to father a kid is beneath even *you*, isn't it?"

"*Excuse* me?" She wasn't sure, but it sounded to her like she shrieked. But that wasn't possible, since she never raised her voice to that extent. A quick scan of the huge room proved her wrong. Every single person was staring at the two of them. Including anyone who'd still been talking when Travis dropped his little bomb. Everyone was giving their undivided attention now.

"Only *you* would consider yourself so superior that you could skip not only the entire human mating ritual but thought you could do the screening and sperm selection all by yourself."

Murmurs started around the room, the sound reminiscent of a fire spreading. Inside she could feel her insides coiling in anger, not to mention the whisper of fear. Dark, slippery, it slithered through her, a thousand memories tightening and threatening to steal her breath. She ruthlessly clenched her teeth, ignoring it.

"Even if I *was* using the experiment for such a distasteful purpose, what business of yours is it?"

"It became my business on the roof," he muttered, finally lowering his voice when it didn't matter at all. The moron.

"You're telling me you were so terrified you might have fathered a child for me that you ran right over to do what, exactly? Talk my uterus out of it? You're a bit past the preventative thinking part of the game, don't you think?"

That stymied him for a second. God, did the man think before he did *anything*?

"I wouldn't worry about it, Travis. My father owns a pharmaceutical conglomerate, remember? I get a birth control shot every three months, just to show my support. You'd be more likely to impregnate one of those lab monkeys you so enjoy playing with." She turned away from him, the sour feeling in her heart returning full force. No wonder the man hadn't had a serious relationship in all the time she'd known him. His ability to speak was only half a degree higher than that of Lassie; with less accuracy. "If anyone should be worried, it's me, what with you screwing your way through the phone book."

"Vetta—"

She waved him off, stalking toward her apartment door,

disgusted. This was ridiculous! He wasn't even right about the experiment—or her—on any level and she was hurt because of it. Hurt! Her eyes were closed to keep the sting of tears from escaping. She could take her mother's absent dismissals of her without batting an eye. Could put up with her father's absent dismissal of *everything* and never think on it again. But Travis Carmichael uttered one word on how little he thought of her and she felt like someone had kicked her ribs in every time. Damn him.

Worse, now thanks to him all those applicants were going to think they had a chance to father a child for her. She could just imagine how many more men would show up hoping they could gain access to the St. Claire coffers for the bargain basement price of a sperm sample.

While more applicants might be a good thing, the reason was galling and insulting. She'd just thrown open the door to the apartment stairway when he caught up with her, clamping a hand around her arm.

"Vetta, dammit, wait."

Angry now, she spun, grabbed him by the shirtfront and shoved him into the stairway before swinging the door shut behind them. A fast slap at the light switch and the overhead fluorescent bulbs blinked on, revealing his unfortunately handsome face. She was tempted to turn them back off, unwilling to let him see the moisture on her lashes. The man would be insufferable if he knew he had the ability to hurt her. So, she shoved her finger at his chest hard enough to push him back.

"Look, Travis, I don't know where you get your information and I don't care what you think about it. This is *my* lab and I do what I please with it. Your sanctimonious opinion of me and my work doesn't give you the right to ruin my results by informing my subjects of any intent, correct or otherwise!"

He did nothing to stop her from making her point, his dark gaze boring into her with messages she couldn't put together. She pulled her hand back to her side, stepping back from him. Somehow, the bright stairwell seemed a very small space and not a smart idea to have dragged him into. Being alone with him was very, very unwise.

"You hate me," she reminded them both when the silence stretched too long.

He didn't respond.

Her heartbeat didn't slow and her body didn't stop that disconcerting reaction to him; her nipples hardening, her belly quivering and that hot swelling feeling making her wet.

"We're not doing this again." Firm. Strong. There was no way either of them would argue with that edict.

Except...he smiled. Not the triumphant grin that had made him countless friends throughout post-graduate school. Not even the smug half lift of the corner of his mouth when he scored a point in an argument. No, this was perhaps the most sexy, sinful expression she'd ever seen on his face—and given she meant Travis, that was saying something. Slowly, like a predator slipping from the reeds, his mouth rose at the corners, giving a hint at the white teeth behind them. His eyes, a rich coffee brown, glittered with intent.

She was screwed.

Or, at the very least, she was about to be.

She must have looked as pleased by that knowledge as she felt because it started like a clap of lightning. He took hold of her, yanking her to him and taking total control of her mouth. Her hips. Her head. *Her.*

His lips were warm, firm, but not punishing. Unlike the

awkward kisses she'd had in the past, she didn't feel suffocated or revolted by the prospect of a man's tongue. She opened wider for him, rewarded by a low groan of satisfaction and the tease of that tongue across hers. He tasted spicy, felt dangerous under her palms, which had settled on his wide shoulders.

That was the last conscious decision she made. She felt the heat of his body against hers, somehow the wall ending up behind her. One of his hands cupped her jaw, tilting her the way he wanted her, and then he took her deep. He slid into her mouth, tasting, caressing, drawing her into a wet, delicious game. She felt his smile, a new sensation she wouldn't have thought could happen. He pulled away, looking down at her with hooded eyes and wet lips, his mouth already forming her name with an awed whisper.

She wondered if she looked that drunk. God, she hoped so.

"I don't hate you." The ugliness of the argument swirled back between them at his words, however gently he said them. "I've done a lot of things to you, but I've never hated you." He squinted a bit. "And you don't have to worry about your health. I'm not quite the man-whore you think I am. I take care of myself and I test. I'm fine and you're fine."

"You don't hate me," she repeated, hearing little else of his small speech.

He shook his head. "But I do want to see you naked," he murmured, his hands gripping her hips, rolling them against his. Two pairs of leggings and some oversize jeans did absolutely nothing to soften the pressure of his erection.

"You've seen me naked," she reminded, a faint grin escaping her guard.

He shook his head. "Naked for *me*."

Vetta looked up the long stairwell to the open doorway at the top. Then she looked to the one so close, just a few steps away. All it would take was a push, a light one, and he'd let her go. It would be over. She wouldn't have sex with him and he wouldn't expect it. She could go back to her lab and her life and her experiment. He'd go back to his, and things would probably be exactly the way they'd always been.

Or she could go up those stairs and change everything.

She closed her eyes, still breathless, trying to clear the fog of sensuality. Did she really want everything to be the way it used to be? Or did she want to feel Travis against her, skin to skin, deep inside her, even just one more time? No one had ever made her feel the way he did. Her body craved that pleasure, the satisfaction she couldn't even bring herself. But would he give her everything she'd longed for, nestled in her bed? Or would she feel exactly as she had last night; emotionally empty, used and sick with herself? She wanted to reach for that lab door, wanted the security of her lonely life.

But she wanted *him* so much more.

"Come with me."

Taking his hand was incredibly easy considering she'd never done it before. The warmed calluses grazed her palm before he twined their fingers and followed behind her. The quiet should have been eerie or frightening. At least, that's what she imagined. Instead, for the first time in her life, she felt completely in control of where her life was going. She was leading the way. She knew what she wanted and she was going to get it.

They walked through the dark living room to the hallway on the left. They passed the pictures on the walls without looking at a single one. She didn't give Jade's room a glance. She kept going until she stood before the closed door of her own room. Grasping the knob, she turned, pushed and walked past the threshold.

Whatever happened now…she'd chosen it.

Travis seemed so much bigger inside her bedroom. He let her go, turning around to inspect, his obvious curiosity probably not satisfied much by the lack of decoration. The space wasn't big, made even smaller by the oversize canopy bed shoved into the corner. Vetta touched the lamp on her dresser adjacent to it. The soft gold glow warmed the room instantly. Everything but her fingertips, which suddenly felt cold without his grasp. Travis looked back to her, a reassuring smile on his face as he sat on the edge of her bed.

Vetta pushed out a breath. "Naked, right?"

"It's a good place to start."

Against her wishes, she smiled. "If the world was fair, you'd have to get naked first. I haven't seen you at all."

"Next time."

She narrowed an eye at him. Then shrugged. Who was she kidding? There was going to be a next time. Probably a lot of them. She shivered beneath her layers, a mental picture of that overwhelming her. Travis…whenever she wanted him. Whenever *he* wanted *her*. Would that be often?

She slid out of her lab coat, letting it drop to the floor behind her. The sweaters weren't easy to shed. She took hold of the lowest one, grabbing it by the hem and pulling it up over her head. She gasped when she felt his hands on her waist, easing upward to help her pull them off. The fabric pile at her feet grew sizably, leaving her in the thin white tank top and bra, but there were still three pairs of pants to get out of. And her shoes. She sighed thinking about it all.

"One of these days you're going to have to tell me why you do this to yourself," Travis murmured, undoing the button on her jeans. A fast unzip and he was slipping his thumbs between her skin and the elastic at her waist.

"No one looks at me this way." That much should have been obvious.

"I've always looked."

She watched his head descend as he worked the jeans, the leggings and her panties down her thighs. It took a minute or so, but he managed to get her free, shucking her socks and shoes with them. Then he whistled soft and low, running his hands up each of her legs as she stepped closer to him. "I never figured I'd find all this underneath, though."

Heat suffused her face.

"All this being something good?" Her mind flashed on old memories, old grainy pictures plastered on tabloids, none of them flattering, always being compared and found desperately lacking.

Travis cocked his head to the side. His brows drew together in question but she couldn't elaborate. Better that everyone forgot about tabloids and bad angles. If he liked what he saw that was all that mattered. She pasted a quick smile on her lips.

His hands slowed their investigation of her limbs. "Hasn't anyone ever told you how beautiful you are?"

A nervous laugh got away from her. "Aside from Jade? I think my mother mentioned it once or twice, but I look more like her than I do my dad, so that's just her being...her."

"Vetta, I'm serious. The other men—"

"Oh, *them*," she interrupted, not at all interested in informing him that his only competition in that department was a funky-shaped dildo. "Do we really have to bring them up? They don't lie as good as you do."

She grabbed the hem of her shirt, prepared to yank it over her head and get back to the business of stripping, but the damn man had to get in the way. He had a fistful of the fabric and kept it exactly where it was.

She frowned down at him. “Are you seriously keeping me dressed so we can talk about what other men I’ve slept with?”

“No,” he replied with a nearly insulting lack of remorse. “We’re keeping you dressed because you know jack shit about talking to people. I don’t lie, Vetta. If I say you’re beautiful, it’s because I mean it.”

She stared down into his dark eyes, registering his affront to the way she’d shrugged off his compliment. She didn’t want to get into a meaningful conversation with him, though. The topic might lead down roads she couldn’t go with him. “Do you have to make everything crass?”

He nodded, not even insulted. “You like me crass. It gets you off.”

“Oh *please*.”

“No, no,” he tsked, flashing his dimples. “That gets *me* off. Hearing you beg is an unfair tactic to getting me away from the subject of *your* fetish—which is good, old-fashioned dirty talk.”

She gave up on her hem to put her hands on her hips. “Me? Beg? You wish. Of the two of us, which one is already on his knees?”

“All the better to hear you from, my dear.”

“What’s that supposed—” Her eyes closed just as they started to roll back in her head. Somewhere between grinning like he’d won something and her question, he pressed his face to her pussy and slid his tongue between the folds. She would have been able to keep the little moan inside if he hadn’t shifted to a sucking kiss, teasing at her clit and making it throb. She definitely couldn’t keep in the snarl of discontent when he pulled away.

He wasn’t in the mood for play when she looked down to

see the intensity in his expression. Cheeks flushed, mouth in a hard line and his dark eyes glowing, she could only catch her breath while he held her hips in his big hands.

“When you’re with me, we’re equal. Neither of us is any better or worse than the other because of how many lovers we’ve had. Sex is best when we can appreciate what the other has to offer. I have more experience. You have a body and a proclivity that I want to explore.”

She itched to squirm. Finally, she felt the urge to cover herself, but didn’t want to give him the satisfaction of knowing it. “How do you know I don’t have more experience than you?”

There was the smug half-lift smile.

“So much for being equals,” she grumbled. “Can I get naked now, please?”

“By all means,” he assented, letting go of her shirt. “Just let me know when you’re done.” Then he pressed his mouth to her pussy again and she had the distinct feeling that equality thing was probably overrated anyway.

There were few things he liked better than hearing a woman come, but there was just something so damn fun about making Vetta do it. She arched her back and made a little sigh of surprise, as if she never felt it building. Every time he heard it, the sound rang like a drug through his bloodstream. He’d moved her to her bed after the first orgasm. She’d never gotten around to taking off her tank top or her socks, but that kind of added to the effect. With her cheeks flushed and her gold lashes down, she looked demure. Pretty unusual sight when her thighs were still laying over his shoulders.

“Your turn,” she murmured, finally lifting her lids to give him a smoldering smile.

“To get naked?”

"That's the way it's supposed to go, isn't it?"

It was if he wanted this to be another wham, bam event. Good as that might feel, he'd spent seven years making plans for Vetta's various tight body parts. He intended to use them. "Here I thought you liked the feel of hard denim on your ass. If I get naked, you're going to miss that."

She pouted. She probably meant to seriously frown but she was too languid to pull it off.

"You're the kind of girl that likes friction." He smiled at her, daring her to get mad. Rising, he let her legs slide to the mattress on either side of him while he moved over her. He let one leg press against her, her hot moisture seeping though the fabric. Her pout vanished as she looked up at him in surprise. Good surprise, though, because she clamped her legs around him.

He had to admit, even this close he couldn't think of a name for the color of her eyes. Beautiful, maybe. Especially when they were warm and her pink lips were wet while she watched him in expectation. The corners of that mouth tipped upward, her small hands plucking at the buttons of his shirt.

"I want to see you."

He purposely raised an eyebrow. "I'm not done looking at you yet."

"You've seen everything—"

He put his fingertip over her lips to shush her. Lowering himself down to lie against her, his leg slid against her puss and his mouth found the lobe of her ear. "I want to see you move, Vetta." He made sure to whisper, just rough enough to make her shiver. "I like to watch you. I like knowing you blush when you come. I want to know what else happens when you try other things."

She released a shuddering breath. He was getting to her

again. A few well-placed words and she went up like a wildfire. Probably not fair to use them against her, but he was no major believer in fairness.

"What other things?" she finally asked from beneath his fingertip.

He smiled, hunger for her going up another notch. "You really want to know?"

Of course she did. But he waited for her to nod before he continued.

"I want to know what your nipples look like in the sunlight. I want to see them get hard when I blow on them." He illustrated by letting his hand hover over her breast. He didn't touch her, but he could see those responsive tips rising to the expected sensation. He put his hand down on her belly instead, earning a frustrated breath from her. "I want to see your hair free. I want to feel it brushing my balls when you ride me."

The frustrated sound grew into a gasp while her hips twitched against his leg. She pulled tighter on his shirt, ripping a button out so she could slip her hand inside. Her touch was warm, fingers splayed across his heart, seemingly unable to decide if she wanted to curl her hand around his neck or continue the trip down his belly. Either one would work for him, but he let her decide to keep caressing up and down until she figured it out.

He closed his eyes, calling up all his favorite fantasies. Vetta on her back, Vetta from behind, on her knees, hell, Vetta in fucking mid-air, if he could figure a way to bend physics.

"I want to see you smile when you're going down on me, wet and noisy."

She tugged his shirt out of his jeans.

"I want to watch you lick me up one side and down the other."

Now both hands were on his button fly. Cool Hand Vetta was making nice work of it too, skipping all the pleasantries for the opportunity to get her hand in there, on his skin, on his cock.

"I'm going to watch you take me all the way down, Vetts. And suck me until you swallow." Dammit, the girl had found gold. She'd shoved everything out of her way and pulled him out, hot and heavy into her hand. That silky smooth hand, just perfect for thrusting against. Shit, if he kept this up he wasn't going to get all the way into a damn thing. Her breathing was fast enough to be only short pants and...and... Fuck it, he needed her. To be inside her.

"You're going to pay for this one," he warned, sliding over her and lining up.

She only laughed. Until he thrust into her. That's when she moaned and raised her hips. Damn but she had fine hips. He wrapped his hands around each one, lifting her hard against him so he could get up on his knees. After that, he lost track of the details. The strokes were long and deep, hard and good. But she surprised him. She didn't just lie there and take it. Not his Vetta. She pushed back, rolling against his thrusts until he managed to reach every inch there was inside her. And she still wanted more.

Looping her arm around his neck, she pulled herself up and kissed him. Hard, wild...best. That was the word for it; best. When they went down again, she landed on top.

It took a minute to get his jeans kicked off, but that seemed to give her a moment to realize she didn't know what to do now that she was in control.

"Ride me," he whispered, pumping up once to give her a hint.

"Wait." Cheeks still flushed, eyes sparkling and her puss

still full of him, she took her time pulling her braid over her shoulder. He gave her another little push, but she just moved slower.

"Vetta," he heard himself growl. She was newer at this than he thought because no one in their right mind just stopped after damn near breaking bones going at it.

But then again, Vetta wasn't anyone else.

She untwined the tie at the end of her hair, then started unweaving the braid. One plait at a time, the warm wheat-colored curls came free. Finally, her arms raised over her head, the long cape fell loosely down her back. Smoky eyes gazed down at him, waiting for him to say something, but damn, speech just wasn't possible. Like a thousand threads of silk, her hair brushed over his thighs, tickling, while tendrils slid over her shoulders and caught the light from the lamp behind her. She looked like an angel. A fiery, golden, sexual angel.

Hell if he didn't have a brand new fantasy.

"Show me what to do," Vetta whispered, closing her eyes and arching her back while she settled on him a little more. The thickness of him still seemed to require adjustment. A deep breath could make her quiver. Those little pulses of him against her walls made her want to move everywhere at once.

"Put your knees down." His voice turned hoarse when she experimented with a little hip roll.

She settled her knees into the comforter, waiting for the next instruction.

"Lift up, just like that. Good. Down again."

She sighed, enjoying the slow surge of him back into her body. He made her feel so full, so...complete. Not that she didn't enjoy it before, with those powerful thrusts that made her want to scream at how good it felt, but there was definitely something to be said for this gentle stroking. Slowly up, slower down.

"Again." The word cost him. She knew it. He said it in a hiss through his teeth. She obliged, letting her head fall back. His knees drew up behind her and she took advantage, using them to lift her body right to the very tip of his penis before gliding back down.

"Fuck me, Vetta," he swore, arching up to be deeper inside.

"I am," she reminded, enjoying each minute movement.

His hands began moving her hips for her, pushing her down from the right, followed by the left, lifting in the same order. She picked up the rhythm, deepening the roll until he groaned. She smiled, more to herself than to him.

"Do you like that?" he asked, hands inching up her belly.

She nodded, concentrating on the sensation of him moving through her wetness. Like hard, hot glass on water. Her tank top eased upward. Absently, she raised her arms to tug it off. But he stopped helping. His fingers had found another pastime, toying with the hard points of her nipples. He plucked at one and her hips jolted forward when she squeaked at the sensation.

"You like that better," he surmised, a smug grin on his face, dimples at the fore.

Not to be outdone, she quickened the pace of her ride. She smiled down into his dark brown eyes, willing him to lose control, but he just smiled back, those white teeth shining and reminding her who the teacher was. Next thing she knew, his thumb was on her clit, skipping any preliminaries and going straight for white-hot bliss.

"You'll like this best."

And God help her, she did. He played with her, lifting his

hips and pumping from below. It was all she could do to stay upright while he thrust and stroked and twisted. She tried to sigh, but she heard herself panting. The pressure began to build inside her, from everywhere, tightening until her body was driving itself—and him—beyond any endurance she thought she had. She had to come. She had to. He wanted her to. She wanted to. And it was so close. So. Fucking. Close.

"Say it, Vetta. Say it and I'll give it to you."

Deeper. God, how was he so deep? So hot and wet. So... So... She shook her head.

"You know you want to." He changed his stroke to her clit and she was washed over in new, shivering sensations. "Say it. What are we doing?"

It wouldn't happen until she did. He'd keep her here, on the edge, just because he could. The word would find its way to her lips because it had already found its way to her pussy, drenching her further while he pumped faster. Her hips eagerly sank down to take him inside, quivering and ready for the final come. But if she was on the edge, he had to be as well and no way was she going to make him feel like he won. So she bit her lip and heard him groan.

"Hurry, Vetta, dammit."

Yes. More, just another... God, yes, yes, yes! "Fuck me, Travis. Fuck me, fuck me." She kept chanting to the time of his thrusts, finally whimpering while he roared his orgasm. She shook, inside and out, the release like a delicious shock of agony and pleasure.

Vetta fell like a limp rag across Travis's chest, heaving in her breath, the wild train ride of his heartbeat thundering in her ears.

Long minutes later, when they'd finally started breathing like people instead of stampeding beasts, Travis wrapped her in his arms and pulled her to his side. Vetta was too boneless to even ask questions, which was great because her brain was too mushy to think of any.

"Sleep," he whispered, smearing a kiss across her forehead.

"I never sleep," she replied. At least, that's what she meant to reply, but he was so warm and his hold so comforting that she had fallen into darkness without even realizing it.

Chapter Five

She woke to the soothing strokes of a rough hand at the small of her back. A smile spread over her mouth and she suddenly understood what it was like to be a kitten. Warm, curled against a comforting body, petted by a steady hand. Of course, this hand had a goal, curving over her butt as if trying to gauge how well it would fit in his hand.

They hadn't bothered with getting under the blankets or turning off the small lamp on her bedside table. Beneath the canopy, though, in that mild yellow light, they were warm enough skin to skin. She burrowed against Travis's chest, her legs tangled with his bristly ones, his heartbeat beneath her cheek, steady and strong. This was what she'd wanted for her first time. This warmth, this comfort. The sense that he cared enough about her to hold her, even if only for a few minutes. She exhaled a sigh, one that felt like it came from her toes. Yes, this was what she'd wanted.

"I have to leave."

Her eyes opened in surprise and before she realized she'd done it, her arms tightened around his waist. "What?"

He made a growly, sleepy noise she recognized. He usually did it when he had to admit he'd done something to her that didn't come off quite the way he meant. Like the time he drilled holes in her test tubes. Her stomach tightened so fast it bordered on painful. She pulled her cheek from his chest and met his slightly guilty expression. He couldn't give her a whole minute with her fantasy, could he?

"Back to your lab?" she asked, hoping she sounded casual. She might not be happy, but it wasn't as if he'd offered anything more than sex. Disappointment was not in the bargain.

"Um, yeah, that too."

"Too," she repeated to herself. Maybe it was the orgasms, but her brain couldn't figure out where else he'd go.

"I... Shit, this would have been easier if I'd told you yesterday like I meant to." His body didn't go anywhere, but she could feel him pulling away in another sense. He looked away and his hand stopped moving on her back. Whatever he had to say, she wasn't going to like it. That much was obvious. She had no intention of hearing it with his hand on her ass.

She pushed at his chest, disentangling their limbs and rolling away from him. She sat up, her nudity more exposing than she ever expected. Her robe hung from the back of her bedroom door, the silk calling like a siren with its brilliant red hue. Telling herself that after what they'd done, watching her walk three feet without a stitch on was hardly going to affect the man, she leapt to the door and snatched the full-length robe. She wrapped it around herself and tied a double knot as quickly as she could.

As ready as she ever would be, she spun to face him and found him sitting up...in more ways than one. Stricken, she tore her eyes from his obvious erection to his rueful grin. "Can't help it if I'm an ass man, honey."

She crossed her arms over her breasts, an effort definitely needed not to look at the thick length all but sitting on his lap, staring at her. "How about you just work on not *being* an ass, then?"

He chuckled. “Can’t make any promises, but I’ll try.”

Well, it couldn’t get better than that, not really. She sat on the chair across from the bed, taking a deep breath while she waited for him to explain himself. And waited. He just stared at her, his stare roving from her ankles to her face and back down. She could only imagine the way he saw her, hair wild and sticking up as well as out; hugging her robe around herself, not a trace of sophistication anywhere near her. His half smile did nothing but make her nervous.

“Travis,” she finally snapped.

He met her questioning glare, shaking himself out of whatever he must have been thinking about. “Sorry, I was...” He cut himself off to scrub his shaggy hair. “I’m leaving town. Moving out,” he clarified with a cough.

If she’d thought her stomach was hard before, the sudden clenching inside felt like something had bitten into her. “Moving where? Why?”

There were more questions, but they were too hard to push through her vocal cords. Had she said something? Gone too far in their last bout of practical jokes? Was he going to move in with one of his various lovers? Her brain automatically tried to ferret out the memory of his last pseudo-girlfriend. The one who did some sort of weird scream thing in Travis’s lab that had frightened Vetta’s own assistants before they realized no one was being murdered. Bitsy? Betsy? Badger? It wouldn’t come, just the memory of the woman’s pillow-flattened red hair as she’d left the lab a few months ago, never to be seen—or thank God, heard—from again.

“My grant’s gone.” Travis interrupted her mental search with an uncaring shrug. “Can’t compete with more effective studies, so no one is biting. I’m out.”

“Broke?” It had happened to their colleagues from time to

time, but Travis had always come through. She'd seen him make do with less money than a panhandler more times than she could remember. He hadn't so much as let her buy him a lunch at those times either. He had the pride of a brick wall and it showed in every hungry line of his body.

Suddenly, the predicament shone in a harsher light. No money to Travis meant no money, period. Possibly negative dollars. "Where are you going to go?"

He shrugged again.

She opened her mouth, automatically about to tell him that he didn't have to leave until he found his feet again, but his dark eyes narrowed to slits of gathering wrath. Her mouth snapped shut.

"So that's my news. That's why I didn't—and still don't—think we should get…involved."

Carefully, Vetta twined her hands together on her lap. "You didn't want me to get attached." As if she had to sleep with him to be attached to him. The man had been a near-daily part of her life for seven years. She knew his voice better than her own. If she let herself, she'd admit to knowing a lot more about him than herself. She'd catalogued so many memories and thoughts about him over the years she no longer bothered to count them. The chasm of his absence opened itself in front of her. Her hands tightened into a double fist.

"I don't want to have regrets when I leave."

"Well…with any luck, *this* won't ruin your plans." She ground her teeth together, afraid to meet his eyes with her own, which were even now filling with tears. She'd known it would happen someday. He'd go, just like her parents regularly drifted in and out of her life. But unlike them, Travis wouldn't be back. Also unlike them, she'd never seen this defection coming. If you could call it that. He'd been her nemesis, probably her best friend by some twisted definition. She should have known he'd go, but still... She felt her tears fall onto the silk covering her breasts.

"See, damn it, this is why I didn't want to tell you."

She half sobbed, half laughed, wiping at her cheeks while he continued painting the air blue and looking for all the world as if he'd committed some sort of felony.

"It'll stop soon." It always did. "It's just the shock."

"I should have told you some better way."

"Travis, honestly." She rubbed her cheek on her shoulder to get the last vestiges of moisture. "Neither of us is capable of tact. It was going to sound bad to me no matter how you put it."

He stopped trying to rub his scalp clean, at least. "Yeah?"

After everything they'd just done, a few drops of truth wasn't going to kill her. "Even if we hadn't...um—"

"Fucked," he supplied easily.

"For the love of—why do you have to bring swearing into everything?" she snapped, her nerves strung tight. "What is the point of making me swear?"

"Probably the same reason I like having sex with you." He winked. "It's never happened before."

Her hands balled tighter. "Travis."

"Why do you like to hear it?" he asked, picking a particularly poor time to be insightful. She responded to his swearing because she liked being reduced to raw need. He was right, no one ever talked to her the way he did, but if she were going to be honest, she had to admit, she just loved hearing the whispered heat of his voice in her ear. It sounded so intimate, hungry. Forbidden. Not much in her life had been forbidden.

Except Travis.

Her cheeks heated against her will. "The point is, I'd still hate to know you're out of my life."

The silence settled between them, making the few feet from her chair to his bare feet at the side of her bed feel like oceans. Even when they were fighting at their worst, they'd never been awkward with each other. But she couldn't push the feeling away. He wasn't even gone yet but he was slipping away. Soon he'd get up and walk out and that would be that. He'd be gone and she'd only have this one night to hold onto. The urge to panic clawed inside her, but she held it in. There had to be a way to keep it from ending like this. She just had to approach it as she did every other problem. Think it through...

"What happens now?" she finally asked, hoping she sounded calm and casual.

He only frowned. "With me?"

"With us."

Horror dawned on his face. "There's an us?"

She rolled her eyes. Nope, he wasn't aware of a thing. "I'm not asking for an engagement, moron. I just meant, what do we do now? Are you leaving tomorrow? Am I going to see you again?"

"Are we going to keep fucking around, you mean?" He always could cut right to the heart of things. She shrugged rather than ask him not to be crude again. He enjoyed making her uncomfortable way too much. He enjoyed making her beg even more.

He grinned, teeth bright, eyes glittering with his usual mischief. "We could see what happens."

"Meaning you'll come over whenever you get itchy and I'm just supposed to be happy about the possibility?" Her pride balked at that. But, then again...

"We always did say you give me the red ass." He leaned

back on her comforter, looking like he was waiting for her to just climb on up. "Hives never sounded so good."

She refused to laugh, but had trouble keeping her mouth from twitching. There could be another way to hold onto him just a little longer. Just long enough to make it easier to let go. If she phrased it right, presented it in a way that would pique his interest...

She shook her head at him. "I have a better idea. Something...mutually beneficial."

He scrunched an eye at her. "The last time you said 'mutually beneficial' we ended up living together."

"Sharing a building hardly constitutes living together." Of course, they *had* spent two years as into each other's business as they could without legal action, so she conceded that he might have a point. "You obviously don't mind having sex with me."

He looked pointedly at the not-quite-out-of-the-way erection jutting between them. "That's fair."

"I'm in need of a lover. You of all people know how difficult it is to find one who is trustworthy."

"Or capable," he added with an almost-weary nod.

She raised her brows.

"Hell, Vetta, you'd kill a lesser man."

She rolled her eyes. "It's nice to know your ego doesn't come into that assessment at all."

"Honey, my ego is always willing to come."

Wasn't that the truth? "So, let's make a deal."

Suspicion finally clouded his smug expression. "If you think I'm going to fuck you just to keep my apartment—"

"Down boy, I'm not that stupid." Though raising the rent would have been an interesting prospect. "But I don't like the idea of you sleeping on the streets, either. How are you supposed to send out resumes or get callbacks? You'll never get back into the field if you fall off the grid."

"I'll get by just fine."

"I never said you wouldn't," she retorted. Honestly. "I'm just saying there's no reason to go simply because the rent is due. Your contract states you have up to three months of nonpayment before I have any recourse. Besides, I don't have time right now to do interviews to fill the other lab and I'd feel a lot safer knowing you're still over there. I count on you to keep that half of the building secure. Your breaking your lease leaves me in a bind. If you stay until you get a direction to go, then that gives me some time to find someone else, doesn't it? At least a few weeks?"

She held her breath, waiting for him to do something other than stare at her like she'd grown another head. Would he see through the ruse? The last thing he wanted was her protection. She couldn't stop him from going—she hadn't been able to stop *anyone* in her life from leaving—but if she played her cards right, she might have more to remember him by than broken test tubes and dirty graffiti on her experiment application.

And maybe, if she spent enough time with him instead of fighting him, she might get a true insight into men, might even figure out what it was about her experiment that was bothering her. She could study him, explore the kind of sex she'd assumed people only read about and make note of what a real man's libido was like. Then maybe when he was gone, she might have a shot at not missing him. If he ran true to form, she'd be glad to be done with him. After all, not one of those women he brought home when he got itchy had ever made a repeat appearance. Yes, this could work perfectly.

If he agreed.

When he finally responded, it wasn't a ringing acceptance. "You stay up late practicing your doublespeak, don't you?"

"I have to. It's the only way I win arguments with you."

His dimple made a brief appearance. "I'll have to keep that in mind."

"Is that a yes?"

"It damn well shouldn't be." But it was. Thank God.

She stifled her relief and moved on to the next phase. "With that in mind, you leaving at some point in the near future doesn't have to mean we end this...*behavior* on principle."

"I thought you didn't want to be my itch-scratcher."

Note number one: Men do listen during arguments. If only to have something to use for ammunition later.

That might be Travis-specific, but she'd make the mental note anyway.

"I don't, not if I don't get anything out of it. I have an experiment to complete, I have no interest in being someone's on-call girl. But that doesn't mean I don't want to continue seeing you."

His suspicion gave way to horror. "As in...dating?"

Vetta sighed heavily. Charting the waters of Travis's phobias was harder than plotting out the galaxy when she was six. "As in a sexual partnership. A *mutually beneficial* one," she reminded. "We meet each other's needs in a variety of ways and when you know where you're going next, it's over. No hearts and flowers, no unnecessary emotional entanglements. Just a nice, clean goodbye. I'd think that would appeal to you."

He nodded, his eyes still narrowed on her. "What I don't get is why it's appealing to *you*."

She heaved a heavy breath. He'd been bound to ask. "Unlike you, who has charmed half of San Diego out of its collective panties, I don't have many options when it comes to meeting my sexual needs. Partners are few and far between." Like…never. "Let's face it, you're as good as it gets for me."

He snorted. "Just for future reference, Vetts, comments like that are *why* I'm as good as it gets for you."

"Then you see my predicament." Helen Keller could have seen her predicament. "I *want* to enjoy a complete sex life. I want to have the freedom to try everything I've ever read about, but that hasn't been possible without a lot of worries; worries that don't apply to you. You won't try to weasel money out of me. You aren't going to sell naked pictures of me to a magazine—"

He brightened considerably. "I get to take pictures of you naked?"

"And you won't tell anyone what we do. In short, I think we can satisfy each other's needs and I see no reason why we shouldn't." Fisted hands didn't shake, so she kept them that way on her lap. She could see the folds of the silk vibrating with her racing heartbeat, but she kept the cool expression on her face that had served her well over the years. If he said no, she'd have her dignity left. And she did still have her toys… Of course, she might have to trade some of them in for a larger size now. She stole another glance at his penis and mentally measured it. Probably something custom-made.

"I have one condition," he interrupted her speculations on girth.

Keeping her relief to herself, she met his level gaze. But his playfulness was gone. In its place was that strange dark expression that made her heart wobble and her pussy clench. Her blood churned beneath his stare and she was unable to tear her eyes away as he stood. So comfortable in his own skin, so beautiful with his rangy grace. He had no idea the effect he had on her. He reached his hand out to hers and pulled her to her feet. His hands untied the sash, parting the red silk so he could cup her breasts.

Vetta pulled in a shivery breath through her teeth when his thumbs and forefingers gently caressed her nipples into hard pebbles sending shocks of pleasure through her. Okay, maybe he had some idea...

"Absolute honesty. None of your little word games, either. Say what you mean, clearly. Tell me what you want and I'll do the same."

She stared, entranced by the hints of gold in his eyes, visible only when they were this close and the light hit them a certain way. His hands slid down and around her back before reaching down to cup her ass. His fingers snaked between her legs, pushing them apart far enough that he could fit the hot and completely erect penis between them. He didn't push himself into her, though she could feel herself soaking him. He slipped between her folds, moving back and forth, but not in.

"When you want a man, you don't have to get creative about telling him. Don't play the ice queen."

"But—"

"When you want a man—when you want *me*—you say one thing and that's it. Say, 'I want to fuck you'. I'll take it from there."

"Wh-what?"

"That's my condition. When you want me, you say it. I. Want. To. Fuck. You."

She blinked, her brain trying to process information while her body couldn't care less. Her hips shifted and he slid through her again, the wide head questing to her now-aching entrance. But still, it wouldn't go in.

This was either the dumbest or the smartest deal she'd made in her life. He could have had any condition he wanted. Her decision was already made. She just had to say the words he seemed to like so much and he'd be hers. For a while, anyway.

"I want to fuck you, Travis."

Note number two: Men like directness. And swearing. Preferably combined.

His answering smile gave her all kinds of dirty thoughts and she realized that for the first time, she'd be able to indulge each and every one of them. It was a heady conclusion. She could either be his puppet or she could pull the strings. Lead him by his nose, if she wanted. Or maybe something else.

A man as feral as Travis shouldn't be so exciting. Or messed with. But she had the inclination to test this newfound freedom. Before he could kiss her, she pushed on his chest and slipped from his grasp.

"I'm going to take a shower." She did him a favor and didn't laugh at his dumbstruck expression. She started toward the door and paused to look over her shoulder. "Are you coming?"

He only took a half second to start after her. "Not alone."

Chapter Six

Travis checked the glowing hands of his watch, wanting to rub the groggy out of his eyes with the opposite fist but it was otherwise occupied. Five o'clock. He groaned in the darkness. It had to be morning. It damn well better be morning. There was no way to know inside Vetta's fortress. Her bedroom in particular had no windows. The few he had in his half of the building were high and in the lab, opened only with an extender and clamp. One sure would be useful because for a full thirty seconds, he had no idea exactly where he was.

It came to him in stages. He wasn't where he usually slept. Which meant he wasn't in his apartment. Which reminded him of why he left his side of the building. Which hopscotched him directly to where he had to be instead. In Vetta's room. In Vetta's bed. And for a delirious number of hours, inside Vetta, herself.

Oh, this was bad. Bad timing, bad decision making, bad karma for all he knew. And yet...panic was not rioting up his spine. The most disconcerting sentiment he could find was contentment.

Definitely time to go.

Too bad he couldn't see a damn thing.

Vetta's body curved into his, filling the wall of his chest with the silky warmth of her back. She held his arm around her, their fingers entwined between her breasts. He dipped his head, breathing in a wisp of the coconut scent he now knew was from her shampoo. For orientation, he told himself, sliding his leg from between hers. Just to be sure where she was so he wouldn't disturb her when he slipped out of the bed. His watch arm was half-asleep, tingling, slow to respond. Actually, not much of him was in a hurry to move. He put it to the softness of her bed, the warmth beneath the blankets and a night of varied sexual activities.

It wasn't like he was a twenty-year-old kid anymore. Once, four trips to Wonderland in a night wasn't a strain on him in the slightest. Of course, in those days he'd been sure to have something to drink nearby. And he'd never been with someone like Vetta, who'd never seen a position she didn't like, which only made him like them all over again. His head throbbed now, reminding him of his last hangover, but it was worth it.

Another sure sign he needed to move his ass.

It took some careful maneuvering, but he tugged his hand free and eased out of the bed. Finding his clothes and dressing in the dark was old hat. Holding his shoes, he opened the door, inches at a time to avoid any telltale creaking sounds. One careful step at a time, he circled the door, pulling it shut with a barely discernible click. Breathing a sigh, he turned in his socks...and jumped halfway out of his skin.

"Eggs?" Jade stood there, holding a cast-iron pan full of fluffy gray stuff. She hadn't turned the light in the hall on, so he assumed that the half light seeping in came from the living room lamp.

"What?"

"How do you like your eggs?" she asked again, reaching with one hand to knock solidly on the bedroom door he'd just shut. He grabbed her hand too late. She tilted her head in question.

"She's asleep." He hoped.

"Really." Why did she sound impressed by that? She pulled her hand free and knocked harder. "Breakfast! Ain't making it twice!"

Travis pulled on her arm again. "Those look great. Why don't we let Vetta sleep and have some food together. Just you and me."

She wasn't fooled for a second. He could tell by the heavy sigh of a breath she let go. She knew a rat when she saw one. Any man who spent the night trying to punch a hole in the wall with a headboard found tiptoeing out of her baby's room before dawn definitely applied. But she let him lead her out of the hall.

"Is there any coffee?"

She scoffed. "You kidding? I gotta keep up with Vetta."

He didn't ask what that meant, because keeping up with Vetta had already changed in his head once for today. He followed behind her, his nose finally noticing the smell of food. A lot of food. Passing through the rectangular living room to the postage-stamp-sized dining area, he could only stop and stare. The small kitchenette table had enough food on it to feed him for three weeks. Pancakes piled high, biscuits, toast, corned beef, potatoes, individual bowls of oatmeal, fruit and three carafes of orange, grape and tomato juice. As he tallied, she added a casserole dish of the eggs from the pan, sprinkled with cheese. Jade turned, expression pleased, no doubt waiting for him to say something. What, he couldn't imagine.

"Oh, coffee, that's right." She turned back to the kitchen counters and pulled a mug from the cabinet above her head, putting it beneath a caterer-sized dispenser. She held the release valve to the side, humming to herself. He hadn't seen one like it since his mother's days as a secretary when he was a kid. It had the glass bulb at the top where the burbling sound and the occasional splash of dark liquid kicked up.

"Is that...a percolator?"

"It ain't coffee if it ain't cooked. Don't you know that?" She brought him his ambrosia.

The smell would have brought him to his knees if he didn't sense a trap of epic proportions. "What's going on, Jade?"

She blinked. "Breakfast. What'd you think it was?"

"It looks like you're up to something."

"A'course I'm up. Not like I could sleep with all that noise." She shrugged, pulling out a chair and settling herself into it, blissfully unaware that he was rediscovering what it meant to feel mortified. "Not that I'm not excited. It's 'bout time you two got together—"

"We're not together, Jade."

The chatter stopped. She raised her head, her gaze boring into him like lasers on kill. "You sleeping with her?"

Since it was obvious, he didn't bother denying it.

"Then you together."

"It's not that simple."

"It is if you stop making it so tough. Sit down and eat. Nothing I hate worse than cold food. *Vetta!*" Her sudden yell was loud enough to make him jump. A mumbled response sounded from the bedroom before a door opened and he saw her stumble into the bathroom. Her ward sufficiently active, Jade leveled him a stare he wouldn't want from his own mother. "Sit."

Manners told him to do what he was ordered. Instinct had him wary of sitting at a table with this woman.

"Don't disrespect my girl by running out on her," she added lowly. "She has enough people doing that, she don't need it from you."

He sat.

Now what the hell was he supposed to do?

Jade began serving onto the dish in front of him and another, presumably, for Vetta. When the woman of the hour wandered into the kitchenette, she was tying the sash on that red robe of hers, her hair tumbling over her shoulders and down her back. She shuffled into her seat, cheeks still flushed, eyes practically glowing. Her mouth had a kiss-swollen look to it. He had to shift in his seat to keep them from knowing his exhausted dick was throbbing a hello at her. It didn't really think it had to make up for lost time all at once, did it?

"You two look...chummy," Vetta murmured, reaching for some toast to dip in her oatmeal. She brushed her hair back behind her ears with one hand, not seeming interested in making eye contact with anyone. The morning-after awkwardness, exactly what he'd been trying to avoid. "What'd I miss?"

"Nothing," Jade replied. She nudged his arm, pointing at his full plate. "You got something against food?"

"Nope. I love to eat, don't I, Vetta?" When she choked on her toast, picking up on his tone, he smiled. She might have the morals of a puritan, but the girl had the mind of a streetwise hooker.

Unfortunately, so did Jade. She smacked the back of his head so hard he nearly dipped his face into the oatmeal. "Not at the table."

"Yes'm." He grinned at her, unable to hold back a laugh. She narrowed an eye, her determination not to sway from her path pretty admirable. For all that he'd charmed her over the years, snitching information and trading favors, he had yet to figure out if he was doing her bidding or she was doing his.

Today wasn't going to be the day he found enlightenment.

She draped a napkin over her lap and sighed, smiling at both of them. "Isn't this nice? Breakfast, just like a family."

Travis's smile died. Vetta finally looked up, meeting his gaze without reservation now, apologies in her eyes. He wanted to tell her it was fine, that he knew what Jade meant, but he wouldn't fool her. It wasn't fine. And he knew exactly what Jade meant.

"Let's just eat. There's a lot to do today for all of us," Vetta said, her pragmatic side overshadowing her shyness. The muscles in his legs ached to get out of there. For her sake, alien as that concept was, he forced them to relax when she murmured, "Please?"

Jade frowned, but she didn't say anything, thank God. He nodded, finally digging into his food. He might not be happy with her, but he'd be an idiot to pass up her cooking. Before he knew it, most of the food on the table was gone. Jade—claiming a diet—only had so much. He took a hearty share, but truth was, Vetta took down most of the meal.

"Does she normally cook this much?" he asked later, helping Vetta clear plates after Jade yawned and headed to her room.

Vetta's color, which had settled to a warm peach, rose once again. She began rinsing in the sink. "She likes to feed me. I only eat once, sometimes twice, a day."

He nodded, bringing over another load from the table. "That have anything to do with her being surprised you were asleep?"

Vetta spared him a casual smile over her shoulder. "I don't sleep very often either."

Travis stopped, turning to her, holding the dish he meant to hand her slightly out of reach. "You some kind of mystic?"

"Hardly." She grabbed the dish from his hold, turning to put it in the sink with the others. "I've read it's common among geniuses. I get a little carried away thinking and forget to sleep. I've never needed much. An hour, maybe two, here and there, if I can shut my thoughts out. It's not a big deal, I'm high energy."

That much he could agree with. "Why is this the first I've ever heard of it?"

Her nose wrinkled when she turned impish. "Strategic omission. I needed every hour I could get to stay ahead of your pranks." She turned completely, looking more like the Vetta he knew so well—eyebrow raised, gaze speculative, mouth pursed—despite the wild hair and svelte body wrapped in silk. "I think this is the longest we've gone without an argument."

He shrugged, heading back to the table for the last of the dishes. "Don't jinx it, I'm exhausted."

She laughed. "Guess you won't be back tonight."

He watched her bend down to lower the dishwasher door. Even beneath the silk, he could see the supple curve of her ass. If he wanted to, he could probably pull the silk out of the way and have a taste of peach. His mouth watered. *Bad idea, Carmichael. She's going to think you feel something you don't if you can't stop screwing her every chance you get.* "No, I won't."

She stiffened.

Way to go, shithead. You hurt her feelings. That alone was hard to admit caring about. He waited for her to turn around, her poker face cemented to her face, before he tried to approach her again. He needed that expression. It kept his pants zipped. At least, until she interrupted his best intentions with words he should have been happy to hear.

"I'm not Jade, Travis. I know what we agreed to. I'm not asking for anything more—"

But he wasn't happy. He didn't want to hear her

reassurances of understanding. He cupped her jaw in his hand, slipping his other one behind her back, cradling her to him until she quieted. He kissed her, a soft, almost chaste kiss, just to reassure her. He wasn't sure he liked how reassuring having her in his arms felt to *him*. It had the strangest resemblance to rightness.

"I meant we can't sleep here again. We'll have to be at my place from now on, because it won't be long before Jade starts bringing us breakfast in bed and I'm sure as shit not going to let her smack me there."

She laughed, a short burst, before slipping her arms over his shoulders and kissing him, not nearly as politely as he'd kissed her. He had to pry himself away. After a while.

"As long as we're clear. We're consenting adults enjoying some time together. It can't be more than that."

Her eyes clouded and her mouth lost some of its upward curve. Finally, she gave a short nod. "I know."

"Good."

So why did confirming with her feel like a mistake he couldn't take back?

ଓ

Vetta sat on the stairs to her apartment, leaning back on her elbows, head falling back, allowing herself to doze. The last fifteen hours had her neck aching, her shoulders tight and her feet throbbing. It was good work, though. The first day's entrants had been prepared for entry into the computer program. There was still one more day of the application stage, and probably another week of program prep. The day's numbers had nearly doubled, no doubt in response to Travis's rash accusation. Tomorrow would be the same. She still didn't like it, but money grubbers running her way was hardly a new experience.

Her first attempted gigolo had snuck into her bedroom when she was fourteen. She never knew how he'd gotten in there, but her mother's Swedish swearwords as she attacked the man with anything breakable she could find had certainly been researched and memorized for future use. She lost count of them long before her eighteenth birthday. Most of them were good-looking, well-dressed, confident bastards. They varied between being obvious about what they could offer and trying to seduce her with oily charm. The good ones were capable of masking their distaste of her dress, her looks, even her barbs. The not-so-good flinched and either fell away quickly or ran for their lives.

Svetlana grew overprotective after the bedroom incident. Penny, sweet, oblivious Penny, did his best to be a vigilant father and hired a security guard. It didn't help much. Either she had no exposure to anyone or she found them everywhere; outside her front door, at restaurants, during lectures. Visits to her mother's vacation spots always guaranteed getting hit on by one or two grinning cabana boys, maybe a couple flirtatious room service men. The smart types who were looking for a shortcut to success generally surrounded her father's pharmaceutical offices or made nuisances of themselves on campus.

Travis spotted them almost as fast as she did after a few years. Once, at a debate, he'd opened by informing the entire audience that her trust fund was sealed until her fortieth birthday. While she'd wanted to strangle him, it did manage to buy her a few uninterrupted weeks.

He'd been the one to see the truth about Rey Del Rio, a classmate of theirs years before. Rey, to date, was the only one who'd slipped under her radar. Travis's surprising warnings fell on deaf ears. It was the one time she wished she'd listened to him.

She'd been assigned Rey as a lab partner and months went by before he made any kind of social overture, even then only for coffee. His animosity for Travis hadn't exactly hurt. Admittedly, Rey lacked Travis's raw sexuality, but he had a grace and dark beauty she'd have to have been stupid to miss. She'd never seen the betrayal coming. His ulterior motives had hurt worse than the others because not one of them actually knew her. They recognized her father's name, to a degree her mother's face. But Rey lied to her face, day after day, patiently waiting for the time to strike. When he did ask her to fund his project, she'd felt stupid in a way she'd never imagined. When she turned him down, he'd threatened to take pictures of her to the press. Rey disappeared without following through, thank God, but she never forgot him. Afterward, she'd decided men weren't worth the space they took on the planet and began investing in plastic toys that could take care of her needs when she had them.

Now, thanks to Travis of all people, toys just weren't going to cut it.

Vetta lifted her head at the sound of the heavy door opening below. Jade entered the corridor, closed the door and started up the stairs. It was slow going—a woman of Jade's girth didn't take stairs quickly or happily—until she came to a few steps below Vetta. Jade stared at her, holding onto the banister with a tight-knuckled grip. No escape left.

Admittedly, Vetta had avoided her nanny all day long. When Jade came down into the lab, her displeasure at the previous night's antics was palpable. Breakfast must not have reassured her about their intentions, either. Travis didn't pop in, didn't call and while Vetta didn't expect him to, Jade clearly did. The older woman's expectations grew heavier and heavier with each passing hour. Jade might put on a smile about the wild sex in the next room, but she didn't approve of flings. Vetta knew better than to think she'd be able to avoid judgment for long.

"He told you about leavin', right?"

Vetta ran her hands over her face to prepare herself for the onslaught. She stayed seated, not quite ready to get up. "Yes."

"On the roof or last night?"

Vetta wouldn't answer even if her hair were on fire. "When did *you* find out?"

"Before he caught you playing Lady Godiva in the living room."

Vetta groaned. *Someone shoot me now.* "Don't tell me he told you—"

Jade waved a dismissive hand. "He ain't the type, you know that. Just figured as much when he came down looking like someone hit him with my granddaddy's old sledge. I know how you are when you think no one can see you."

Vetta left her cries to God safely echoing in her head so Jade wouldn't mistake them for requests for help from *her*. "Why on earth would you send him up there knowing what he might walk into?"

Jade gave her a look. "I never made it secret I hoped you two would get together. Not my fault you can't take a hint."

Of course not. It was never Jade's fault when things happened exactly the way she planned them. Vetta sighed, but the weight in her chest didn't lighten. "Seeing me naked is not a hint, Jade."

"You two are dumber than most." Jade raised her foot to go up another step, groaning as she did. Vetta stood up, pressing her back to the opposite side to give the older woman all the room she'd need. Three stairs higher, Jade paused, turning enough to meet Vetta's gaze. "What do you think? Is he really gonna go?" Her voice stayed soft, vaguely worried. This time, there was a hint of maternal sadness as well. Jade would miss Travis too, whether he knew it or not. Knowing him, he wouldn't even guess how much he mattered.

Vetta hugged herself. He wouldn't think *she* cared either. "I...I don't really know what I think yet."

"You don't want to do something for him?"

Vetta scoffed. If only it were that easy. Look how hard it had been to convince him to stay when he was still entitled. "Travis won't take anything from me. He's got all that stupid male pride, for one thing. There's no way he'd let himself owe me anything. And if I was dumb enough to offer him anything it would sound like begging to keep him here."

"What's wrong with that?"

Vetta eyed Jade, making sure she hadn't lost her mind. "I am *not* begging him to stay."

Jade leaned her back against the left wall, using the end of her headscarf to fan her face. "Looks like he ain't the only one with pride."

"Fine, I have pride. Happy?"

"You married?"

"No."

"Then I ain't happy."

Vetta listened to the rustle of Jade's dress, the pitch of her breathing in the echoing hallway as she made her way up the remaining steps. That was why she didn't have a door at the top. Jade generally got around the apartment and the lab fairly easily. It was getting from one to the other that worried Vetta, so she made as few obstacles as she could.

She was originally going to put in an elevator, but Jade had insisted she needed the exercise and twice daily through the "Torture Chamber" was good enough for her. It wasn't, not really, but it was all Vetta could get her to do.

Vetta smiled, despite herself. Jade's evil plan to marry her off to Travis had started somewhere around the first time Vetta mentioned him at home. She'd known him two days and didn't like that prickly feeling his gaze gave the back of her neck. It was like she could feel him staring or something. Jade insisted the feeling was attraction. It felt more like acupuncture.

When Vetta had explained about giving Travis first refusal of the extra lab, Jade thought she'd admitted to some secret crush. Ever since, Jade had made it her goal in life to throw them together as often as possible while she stayed unobtrusively—not to mention inculpably—in the shadows. All that ever came of it were new arguments, new pranks and new scores to settle.

Until now.

Travis's misinterpretation of the ad was as accidental as dropping the H-bomb. About as subtle, too. "Why did you tell him I was using this experiment to find a sperm donor?" Vetta faced the open doorway where Jade suddenly had a coughing fit. She hurried up the steps, putting an arm around her friend and guiding the older woman to the large beige couch in the middle of the room. They sank into the oversize pillows together, Vetta clapping hard on Jade's back.

"Water?" Jade asked through teary eyes.

Vetta nodded and went into the adjacent kitchen, quickly getting a glass from the drain board and filling it at the tap. It was only after she turned off the faucet that she noticed there was no coughing any longer. She walked around to the living room again, her eyes narrowing on her now evenly breathing roommate.

Jade blinked back.

“How much of that was real?” Vetta held away the water.

“How much is going to get me busted?”

Vetta rolled her eyes. “What am I going to do with you? You’re supposed to be taking care of me, not giving me coronaries.”

“You worry too much and I *am* taking care of you.”

“By lying to Travis and telling him I’m looking for someone to father my scientifically enhanced love child?”

“Got him over here, didn’t it?”

There was simply no castigating a person who refused to feel guilty. “You can’t change anything this time, Jade. Please, let me handle this relationship on my own.”

“You mean end it,” Jade grumbled, her face fixed in a deeply grooved frown.

Vetta could only shrug, painful as the truth was. “It’s what he wants.”

“What do *you* want?”

She handed Jade the glass of water. Then she walked out of the living room. If she had an answer to that, the last person she could share it with was Jade.

Chapter Seven

"Interested in a grand tour of my lab?" Travis asked, leaning on the wall next to his door as Vetta ushered the last applicant out of the building's main doors. She had to hold in a sigh at the sight of him, not that she wasn't used to that. It was the welcoming, wolfish grin on his face she wasn't accustomed to. He'd leaned his rangy body in a casual pose, his feet in their scuffed tennis shoes crossed at the ankles, arms crossed over his chest. For all intents and purposes, he was the most relaxed man on the planet. And the sexiest. And he was offering her another night of sensuality.

She turned the lock on the glass doors and pulled out the key, jangling the rest against her leg. "Is that the scientist's version of, *wanna come see my etchings?*"

He chuckled as she walked closer. "No, that would be, *wanna come see my electron microscope.*"

"You should have tried that one, gets me every time."

"How about, *I'll show you my Petri dishes if you show me yours.*"

Vetta's scientific interest perked up. "You'd show me your samples?"

Travis's teasing grin disappeared. "What do you want with my samples?"

Well, that was smart. Get the man thinking you're after his research. "I've always been interested in what you do in there." The few times she'd ever been allowed inside had inspired a near-violent curiosity she'd never allowed herself to indulge. If she'd asked about his work even once, he'd have either clamped his already-tight lips or teased her mercilessly with pointless clues just to get her wondering. "When you're alone, that is." God knew he'd had enough women come and go to need clarification.

"Liar. You're curious when I'm not."

She wasn't admitting to that one. Since it occurred to her this might be her last chance to see his work, she decided to see how she might make use of his own hard-to-control desires. "What if I let you choose how I say please?"

Suspicion disappeared. In its place, she could see the wheels of his dirty mind beginning to turn. "Any way I choose?"

Dangerous territory. He had a wicked imagination. She shivered, heat blossoming low in her belly as she remembered the various ways he'd already used it on her...inside her... She'd created a file on her laptop with notes from her memory already. She could always use more pages. There wasn't a downside to this bargain. "Provided I don't need medical attention afterward, sure."

"You don't know what you're missing out on." He mocked disappointment, but reached for her hand and pulled her to the door, then beyond.

She looked around his lab, noting that it was quite sparse when compared with hers. There was no receptionist's desk and so much open space that shadows took up more room than the furniture. There were three long tables, each one covered with either microscopes, computer equipment, paperwork or books. Against the far wall was a bank of faintly glowing refrigerators with glass doors. Vetta didn't need to explore to know that was where he kept his cell cultures. She turned back to him, her right hand idly rubbing under her own chin with thought. What could he be up to? No other way to find out—aside from snooping—other than to ask.

"What are you working on?"

Travis walked to the first table with a sigh. "Nothing, now."

He couldn't possibly think that would satisfy her. "What *was* it?"

He shook his head, a strain showing at the corners of his mouth. "I don't want to talk about it."

Normally, that was her cue to back off. She might even have listened, as she did whenever she trampled too close to things he held precious. But something about his reticence was different. Less that he was angry. More like if he simply couldn't bring himself to speak. "If it bothers you this much, maybe you should."

"I didn't invite you in to talk, Vetta."

That much, she knew. "No, but you did intimate I'd get to look around. Since when have you known me to look and not ask questions?"

A grinding sound accompanied the tightening of his jaw.

Okay, new angle. "You can at least tell me why you don't want to talk about something you've lived and breathed for years."

Whatever patience he had disappeared. Even the erotic promise of their discussion in the hall evaporated. Now he was back to being her adversary. It was a change she found she didn't want or appreciate. "You wouldn't understand."

She felt herself automatically bristle. She'd heard that for years, usually said by some man who didn't understand whatever he was talking about, either. She'd never heard it from Travis. Reminding herself that temper hadn't gotten any answers from him before, she made an attempt to reason with him. "Why wouldn't I understand? I'm smart, remember? Understanding problems is what I do."

He shook his head and turned away from her, mumbling words she considered herself lucky not to be hearing. Inside herself, nerves began to pull taut. Instincts demanded retreat. Her emotions, on the other hand, gave her courage to stay.

"Travis." If she thought he'd let her, she'd touch him. Soothe the hard lines of his shoulders. Indecision kept her rooted and silent.

Travis seemed to struggle with something, a shudder rippling the tension in his shoulders, before answering, his voice low and angry. "You wouldn't understand because you've never failed anyone."

She drew back, confusion an emotion she liked even less than indecision. "Fail? Who did *you* fail?"

Some men walked away when conversations became things they didn't want to deal with. Not Travis, he always stood his ground as long as he could. She could see his irritation hitting new highs, but he didn't walk away or throw her out. Instead, his shoulders hunched as he braced both hands on the table and leaned across it, his bowed head facing away from her.

"My mother never wanted anything else but to see me graduate. See me do something with my degree and she didn't get to. I haven't done anything in the two years that I've been on my own to make her sacrifice worthwhile, either. Look at this place!" He gestured broadly at the vast emptiness with an angry swipe of his palm. "Would you be proud if you were her?"

Vetta followed the scope of his gesture. From the refrigerators to the files and the books and computers. It was modest, some would even call it all eclectic, but there was nothing there that should have brought him shame. All she could see was his work, his sacrifices, his very life, laid out in page after page of research. Even as his enemy, much less as a mother, if someone had asked that question, there would be only one answer.

"Yes," she whispered, the word escaping like a breath.

He lifted his head, turning enough for her to see his profile as he worked his jaw. "Don't lie, I'm not blind."

"Neither am I." Her insides trembled but she quelled it. "You've managed on a shoestring for two years, Travis. Longer. You have top-of-the-line equipment, you're at this night and day. You've got the degree, you're *doing* the work. You did what she wanted, what you *both* wanted. She died knowing you would. That was enough for her or she'd still be here beating you up to do something with your life."

The only sound in the echoing lab was her own gasp for breath.

Ten interminably long seconds later, he chuckled, a dry humorless thing. "God I wish she'd met you. She wanted to, you know. Said even then I should stop pulling your braid and kiss you."

Oh, she could just imagine his response. But her curiosity got the better of her. "What did you say to that?"

Vetta waited and wondered once more about the woman who had raised him. She'd seen her once, across a quad, as Travis showed the woman the various buildings. There wasn't a lot to glean from the woman's looks. She'd been pretty, her coloring much like Travis's. She'd seemed down to earth, her thick blonde hair pulled back into a ponytail, her arm looped through Travis's while they talked and walked and seemed oblivious to anyone else around. Until Travis had turned her way, their gazes making contact as they always did no matter how far from each other they were. She'd turned back to her books as fast as she could, shaking for reasons she hadn't been able to decipher. Later, especially after his mother died, Vetta couldn't seem to stop wondering what would have happened if she had held his gaze. Would he have brought his mother to meet her? Would the late Mrs. Carmichael have liked her? Or was it for the best that they'd never had to vie for Travis's attention?

"That doing so would result in her having that daughter she always wanted." His answer snapped her out of her errant thoughts. He rubbed his face, wiping his aggressiveness away, but the weariness remained.

She knew that weariness. It was born of regret. Inside herself, Vetta felt the weight of his disappointment. All his work, all his dedication. She should have known what he was working on without being told. "Your experiments. They're about her."

He nodded. "She died of ovarian cancer, did you know that?"

She nodded. He'd been inconsolable after the funeral. Maybe destroyed would be a better word. The first time she'd cried in years had been his first day back. He'd looked at her as if she weren't there. As if *he* weren't even there. And there had been nothing she could do but wait until he'd come back to himself. Even then, he was different. Losing his mother had changed him completely. She just never realized how much.

"She died almost before she knew what hit her. All my life, she worked to make up for the things we didn't have. She gave up so much just so I'd have the best education and tools she could get. When she got sick, she worked through it, to finish my tuition fees and never even mentioned it to me. Said that the doctor told her there wasn't much to be done by the time they discovered it anyway. She didn't want me to miss any school nursing her when I was so close to my degree. Didn't want to *distract* me."

His bitterness kept even Vetta's mouth closed.

He sighed, heavy and pained. "I wasn't expecting to find a cure all by myself. I'm not that obsessive of a zealot. But I thought maybe I could make a difference in the research. Look in places where others haven't tried yet. I wanted to search the nooks and crannies and, at the time when I started, they hadn't even scratched the surface of estrogen research. I thought I'd make a difference."

Was he assuming he hadn't? What if his work had enabled others to be approved? And why did he sound as if he didn't know he had more to do? Her brows knit, but she knew he had more to say. "Sounds noble."

He shook his head. "No, it sounds ridiculous. At least to all the grant boards I've submitted to in the last year. A few years ago, the subject was obscure enough that being funded was the medical science field's idea of covering their bases. Now there are thousands of groups turning their attention to estrogen and hormone replacement. No one has funds to waste on a one-man operation. I can't even blame them for it. I simply have to face facts. I haven't published enough, I don't have promising enough results to report and I don't have a fast enough deadline to achieve them." He glared down at the table of equipment and all the individual pieces as if they were dead plants instead of impressive microscopes. "It's over."

Vetta stared at him, disbelieving. Wasn't he the man who never quit, at anything? Wasn't he the one who pushed his body to the breaking point on the football field for a collegiate education? Wasn't he the one who worked any job he had to in order to make tuition? Wasn't he the one who would starve for days at a time to keep the work going? What had happened to *that* man? “Why are you giving up so easily?”

It was the wrong question to ask. She saw it in the leap of muscles at his shoulders, just before he pushed away from the table and faced her, flushed with anger.

“*Easy*?” he asked, his voice echoing in the lab like a rifle shot. “Who are *you* to accuse me of doing anything easy? You have no idea what it’s taken me to keep my research going. You go around doing whatever comes to mind, never considering what it takes anyone else to do real, meaningful science. You’ve had everything handed to you on a platter and when there’s absolutely nowhere left for me to go, *you’re* telling me I’m giving up too easily? Who the hell do you think you are?”

She stared up at him, not surprised in the least by his outburst. She’d heard sentiments like it a thousand times before. Sometimes even from him, though never so harshly. Still, she’d always known what he thought. What everyone thought. But they were wrong.

“Nothing in life is easy. For everything you get, you lose something else. Absolutely nothing comes without cost, Travis. Even for me.”

“Yeah, and what have you lost, *Solstråle*?”

It was tempting to walk out right then, to let him sour in his low opinion of her, to leave what could have been exactly where it was. But they’d both done that too many times. She couldn’t make her feet pick up and go. Not this time.

“More than you can possibly imagine.”

He raised his chin, his silent accusations blaring in her ears.

“Self-respect, for one thing. Self-confidence. Usefulness. It’s easy, giving up. You get to be relieved from the effort of trying. You get to walk away and pretend to yourself you might just come back and give it a shot some other time. But you won't. You know you won't. And you quit anyway. If you do that, *then* you've failed. Not one second before."

He only glared in response.

"You're quitting and that's not like you. You won't want to live with yourself if you do it, believe me, I know."

"You'd have to start something to quit it, Vetta," he finally responded, his voice low and resentful.

"No, you don't." Painful, how true that was. "It's more than possible to give up long before you start anything at all. Why do you think it is that I don't do any of your so-called meaningful science?"

She leaned the small of her back against his table, facing him across the few feet between them and crossing her arms over her chest the way he was so prone to doing. She waited for him to put it all together.

Instead, he merely frowned at her. "What are you talking about?"

Well, she should have known better than to assume he'd do the math in his current mood. "Psychology. I'm a product of my parents' various mistakes the same way you are a product of your mother's hard work and good intentions. They didn't mean to make my life difficult, but being their daughter put me in a bad position from the get-go and they weren't the types to imagine fame as a detriment. But it was. My first steps were on a Barbara Walters' special. My first acne breakout landed in a fashion magazine because they were doing a layout with my mother and she brought me along for the shoot. You don't even want to imagine what happened the first time I wore a bikini."

"Vetta—"

"I couldn't handle it, Travis," she said sharply, cutting him off and leaving him bewildered. "My mother was—still is—the epitome of the male sex fantasy. Every day I was compared to her and found not only lacking, but not even worthy to be called her daughter."

"But you were just a little girl," he interrupted, compassion coming easily to him.

She shrugged because compassion had never been a close personal friend. "It didn't matter, not to the press. I tried to hide as much as I could under more and more clothes, but they would just take more pictures and report how I was gaining weight. Before I knew it I was Svetlana Swinton's fat daughter. They took pictures of us through our windows, in our home, for Pete's sake. There was no escape. I figured, looking horrible wasn't enough, I had to *be* horrible through and through. I made it a point to get good at making people feel small and stupid."

"Really good," he agreed a little too appreciatively. He finally lost his frown to drop her a sheepish grin.

"Even the most dedicated of paparazzi don't like to be outsmarted or humiliated publicly. After a few years, most of them disappeared for the flashier and more willing celebrities. I got to study in peace." She eyed him and shook her head. "For the most part. Now all I have left are the people after my father's money. But can you imagine what might happen if anyone got wind that I might be anything more than a spoiled, overweight, trust-fund princess? If I ever published something *meaningful*?"

The implications must have become clear suddenly.

"So, you never even bothered to try? You just..."

"Quit," she said for him, taking no pleasure from the slack-jawed shock on his face. "Oh, I've had ideas and even some brief studies, but I've never done anything with them. I've just contented myself with providing for people who were able to do the work I can't."

"The work you *won't*."

So much for slack-jawed.

At her curt nod, he went back to being angry. "It's a waste, Vetta, an even bigger one than I ever knew. Don't you see the difference a mind like yours could make?"

She shook her head. He didn't get it. Once again, he was the one who didn't understand. "I'm doing what I'm able to do by directing others. I'm not going to dive back into public consumption, no matter what you think of me for it. Believe me when I say that failure on a global scale is nothing you've ever experienced, even if it feels that way right now. If you really do give up and fail, the only ones who will ever know about it are you and me. You can recover. Anything I fail at now..." She held back a shudder. "I'm not prepared to handle another lifetime of wide-scope ridicule. I quit while I was ahead."

"Behind," he corrected.

"Whatever. The choice was made a long time ago and I've had to deal with that. You're about to make the same decision and you don't have to."

He sighed, she hoped with some touch of comprehension. "That's not what I'm doing. I've simply run out of road."

"You haven't asked *me* for more road." The words were out before she could stop herself. Inwardly, she braced for rejection.

Travis didn't disappoint. "I'm not going to, either."

"Why not?" Her mother had said more than once that her addiction with the word *why* was her worst quality. Travis's obvious exasperation probably meant he agreed.

"I just told you about me and my mother. I'd think it'd be self-explanatory."

"Please do not get me started on your use of the word think."

That earned her a hard glare.

She rolled her eyes. "Sorry, habit. But it doesn't change the fact that you're wrong. I was there, remember? Your mother didn't work herself sick any more than you did. You both put you through school, worked harder than anyone else I saw there. You shouldn't rob yourself by thinking you don't deserve the degree you got. If I gave you a grant, you'd earn that one just the same."

"I won't take handouts."

"I fund hundreds of independent studies. What makes funding *you* a handout?"

He fixed her with a dark glare she didn't know he was capable of. "You aren't sleeping with any of them."

"Should I remedy that? Maybe go pay a house call to every lab from here to Maine?" she asked with a dark look of her own. "I can't take back what we've done, but it hardly has any bearing—"

"You weren't tripping all over yourself to give me money before."

"You weren't asking for any before," she reminded.

"I'm not asking for it now." That statement seemed to reassure him of something because his grim bearing faded, but the tension in him remained. "Which reminds me. You haven't said please yet."

She blinked at the sudden change of topic. "I'm not done—"

He stalked toward her, stopping only when she had to look up at him, her back pressed to the edge of one long table. He leaned farther still, a slow, calculated grin spreading over his lips when she curved backward to keep the spare inch between them. "Yes, you are."

She shivered, her body responding predictably. Her breath

caught, her skin warmed and the tingle of excitement began to dance low in her belly. "You can't shut me up with sex."

"Maybe not, but I can sure come up with better things to do with your mouth." His kiss wasn't gentle or seductive, but it dragged her in anyway. With one fierce hold, he could possess her and take total control. His hips pressed against hers and when she raised her hands to push him away, he took control of them as well. Their fingers twined while Travis pulled her hands to his own waist. It didn't occur to her to do anything but follow his direction and hang onto him. Before long, she was all but lying back on the table, a microscope-base corner pushing against her temple and an open book making a disturbing rending noise beneath her back.

The kiss, though, was worth it.

She let him lead, let him almost punish. He wanted her quiet. Wanted her to stop saying things he wasn't ready to hear. Or maybe he didn't have the heart to hear. She wasn't sure, but she let him. It wasn't even hard. She just closed her eyes and held on until his lips softened, until his hands left the edge of hurting, leaving only a sweetness, only solace in arms that had turned from a trap to a cradle.

Travis lifted his head, peering down at her. "What is it about you that changes everything I plan to do?"

Not everything, she knew. There was nothing she could do to keep him with her. She had the urge to reach up and touch the hard edge of his cheekbone and hold onto the comfort a little longer. If her hand wasn't tucked beneath his arms, she might have done it, but the notion felt more tender than he would probably allow. He wouldn't like her even thinking anything tender, despite the kiss or the strange expression on his face. As if he didn't quite recognize the woman beneath him.

She didn't quite recognize herself. Two days ago she'd have

kneed him in the crotch if he'd dared to try to kiss her quiet. Now...now she only wished she could snuggle closer. She tried to smile and shrug the sentiment away, hoping he didn't notice the tremble she felt coursing through her.

He must have, though, because he slowly retreated, slipping away from her. Vetta sat up, waiting for him to make his exit. He'd make some kind of joke, maybe some flippant insult to make her pick a fight, because she'd crossed too many lines in one encounter. Stupid. She'd known his rules for years. Never get involved. The women he was with before were always blatantly temporary. If he knew more than their first names, she'd have been surprised. Vetta began calculating instances when she'd revealed caring. There were too many of them and she could see him doing the calculations as well.

Except he didn't send her away.

He looked as confused as she was. "What am I supposed to do with you?"

Better to let it pass before he gave in to his flight instincts. "If you need ideas, I have a whole shelf of instruction manuals."

He heaved in a breath, the corner of his mouth twitching, then reached forward to pluck her hand from her lap and pull her off the table. "Come on." He led her to the internal stairwell, making good time to the top. He ushered her through the final door to his apartment, closing it behind her with an anticlimactic click.

Vetta looked around, blinking. "It's a cave."

Travis put his hands in his front pockets. "I know."

She couldn't believe it. Wall to wall, nothingness. Nothing on the floor to cover the stark slab of concrete. Nothing on the walls to break the seamless flow of white paint. Not even a cover for the exposed double-bulb light fixture in the center of the ceiling.

"It hasn't changed since I first showed it to you." She'd meant to leave it wide open for him to make it his own. It never occurred to her he would leave it that way.

She saw his nod in her peripheral vision. "I know."

She turned her head to deliver a baleful glare. "This probably makes me judgmental and evil...but this is sad, Travis. Even for you." At least he had furniture. Sort of. His abominably ugly black recliner and a coffee table that had gouges and scratch marks all over the matte surface, most likely from his feet. There were a couple of other tables. One had a small TV with a pair of rabbit ears duct taped to the wall above it. The other had a phone/answering machine combination and a notepad on it. An aluminum dinner tray balanced next to the recliner. His dining room area had shelves but no table. She gave him points for full shelves. From the few feet away, it wasn't hard to see they were research materials. She doubted he had any leisure reading around. If anyone needed something to relax him, it was Travis.

Unless that's what the women were for.

"I never needed anything more than this. I keep most of my paperwork in one of the bedrooms as an office. The other one is for file storage."

"So where do you sleep?"

He pointed at the chair.

Vetta stared at it. It had once been leather, she decided. Maybe pleather. It had long ago lost any texture...or comfort, if she didn't miss her guess. The arms were worn and torn in places. The armadillo design of pillows overlapping pillows for the upper portion of the seat was flattened like pancakes. If she looked hard, she could probably see Travis's exact imprint from his feet to his big, stubborn head.

He circled the arm of the chair, dropping into it. He smiled up at her and patted his thigh.

Vetta eyed the denim over his leg for any kind of irritation. There didn't seem to be any insects. Maybe a flea?

"Vetta?" He patted again.

Her neck tightened. She brought her hand to her throat, feeling around it with the tips of her fingers.

Travis tilted his head. "What are you doing?"

"Feeling for a collar. Or some fur. There's got to be something here if you think I'm going to come running because of a hand pat." She gave him a glare that should melt steel. "Don't confuse me with one of your Pavlovian lab monkeys. Especially not the redhead who couldn't stop screaming."

His brow creased. "Pamela?"

"Whatever!" Great. Now she had a name for her auditory trauma.

"Vetta."

"What?" she all but growled, wishing she could get that woman out of her memory. Get all the women out. It wasn't that she thought she had any real claim to him. Just that they were a testament to his need to be free. He never slept with women who mattered. Logically, it was smart to remind herself of that not-so-subtle fact.

For the first time in her life, she hated logic.

"Shut up and get your ass over here already."

The moment didn't last long. "Gee, when you put it that way... No."

He looked as mutinous as she felt. They'd planned to have uncomplicated sex and from the second she saw him in the hall it had been anything but. Why wasn't it uncomplicated?

Note number eighty-five: Men claim to be simple creatures, yet they manage to make everything simple into an argument.

"You're forgetting the deal, Vetts. We're supposed to be honest at all times. I'm supposed to tell you what I want, remember? What I want is for you to come over here and sit with me."

"Oh, I remember. But you should remember that wanting and getting are completely separate things. One does not ensure the other."

"Especially where you're concerned," he grumbled. She thought he muttered something that sounded like "twenty-two to *seventeen*", but couldn't be sure, since that made no sense at all. When she leaned forward suspiciously, his hand shot out and grabbed hers. A solid yank had her spinning into his lap in a sprawl.

She used her elbows to sit up, caring little when he shifted rapidly to avoid the hard points. "What lesson is this supposed to be? Never take no for an answer?"

He grinned. "Don't be afraid to take what you want." His hands began tugging on her lab coat. "I've got to get you to stop wearing so damn many clothes."

The jacket came off, but he still had three sweatshirts and two T-shirts to get through. "Consider it my way of requesting foreplay."

He stopped moving, narrowing one eye at her. "Is that supposed to be a dig at my technique?"

It was nice to be wanted so much a man that he was tearing to get at her. Plus he deserved it for dragging her into her current position. She lowered her lashes the way she'd seen her mother do countless times. "What technique would that be?"

"If you don't watch it, it'll be Paddleball."

She grinned at him. His lap really was pretty comfortable. She wriggled closer to him.

Travis's gaze turned accusing. "You're enjoying this."

"Didn't you want me to?"

"I wanted you undressed first." Should she tell him he was almost pouting?

Vetta leaned back and decided not to fill him in. Teasing was a lot more fun. She swung her feet on the other side of the chair arm a few times. "Who's stopping you from undressing me?"

He tugged at her sweaters. "That would be you."

"Haven't you ever heard that saying, *anything worth having is worth working for*?"

"No, I'm more your *anything worth doing is worth doing well* guy."

Yes, he was, the smug schmuck. "Well, I'm waiting. Do something well."

"Always did like a challenge." He started with a sweater, pulling it from the others and getting it over her breasts before she started laughing and pulling it back down. He gave it another few tugs before he was laughing with her. "Damn, Vetta, you could get an easy-unlock zipper or something. I'm gonna need a hacksaw to get you out of these things."

"You're the one planning to have sex on this godforsaken chair. If either of us is demanding the impossible, it's you."

"I thought you wanted to try everything."

She tried to get a little of her sarcasm back, but she was feeling too light. Too happy. "Are you claiming that my experiences won't be complete unless we do it on a beat-up recliner?"

"No, but I'll be able to check it off *my* fantasy list."

She stilled his hands with her own. "Since when have you fantasized about me?"

He didn't want to answer that one, she could tell. But she wanted to know. When he moved his head to look away, she touched his chin and drew his gaze back to her own. "Tell me."

"I just know I'm going to regret this, but it won't hurt anything to tell you now, I guess." He brought a fingertip to her lips, tracing the shape and parting the bottom from the top. "I had my first fantasy about...ten seconds after I met you. You were passing my seat on the step in the lecture hall and snagged your foot on my bag. You didn't fall but your mouth... It made this perfect 'O'. I've never forgotten it."

Vetta forced herself not to purse her lips for him now, the flesh of her lips tingling beneath his touch. "Why didn't you say anything?"

"You were *twelve*."

She rolled her eyes. "I was *eighteen*."

"Barely. Believe me, the last thing I had time for was a virgin with stars in her eyes."

Vetta started, the sensual spell around them breaking. "You say that like being a virgin is a bad thing."

"No, virginity is fine. But virgins generally get it in their heads that the first man they sleep with is their one true love or some other kind of bullshit." He had no trouble rediscovering his dry sarcasm. "I'm no one's Prince Charming."

Note number eighty-six: Virginity is a turn-off.

Vetta nodded, more to herself than in understanding. "Is this a common thinking among men?"

"I can't speak for all of mankind or anything." He chuckled, then seemed to realize he's said something wrong because he sobered fast. "Anyone committed to their goals who isn't a selfish bastard would avoid a virgin as best he can. It's only common sense." He turned his head to study her. "Are you making mental notes?"

Uh oh. "Why would I do that?"

"'Cause you have that look. The one that says you're filing something away for later."

That made her smile. "You've catalogued my expressions?"

"Know thine enemy. I figured out a lot about reading body language on the football field. Saved my ass more than a few times, let me tell you." He smiled, seemingly to himself, probably over all kinds of situations.

Well, that explained plenty. He'd escaped most of her traps by reading her physical cues. Did that mean he'd always know when she was keeping something from him? The last thing she wanted was to fill him in on her sexual status. If virginity was a turn-off, deflowering was probably a complete ball-breaker.

He refocused on her, as if something just occurred to him. "What do you care about virgins, anyway?"

Nope. Definitely not telling him.

Luckily, she knew Travis probably as well as he seemed to know her. He'd caught the scent of her thoughts. He needed distracting.

His thumb was still poised just beneath her bottom lip. She pulled back only far enough to purse her lips around the tip. "Was it like this?"

His gaze flickered, interest in the chocolaty depths. "Was what like this?"

She let her lips soften, inverting the caress. "My mouth. In your fantasies. Was it anything like this?" She smiled around his thumb. Remembering a scenario from one of her erotic books, she flicked out her tongue to touch him. "I never did get around to saying please."

His eyes narrowed and the hint of a flush reddened his

cheekbones. She looked again, raising her lashes slowly. The corner of his mouth rose at the same pace.

Distraction complete.

"In my fantasies, you're not licking my hand."

"In your reality, I don't have to be either."

"Will you be naked?"

"Is that what you want?"

He nodded. Her heart began thudding as excitement took over. Vetta decided then and there that saying please wasn't as bad as she remembered. She stood, pulling the coat off his lap as well. Habit made peeling away the layers of clothing easy. The sweaters she tossed behind the chair. Feeling frisky, she pulled off the tees one at a time. Until there was only the lace-edged bra left.

She unhooked that from between her breasts and peeled it away from her skin. His hungry gaze roved over her like hands, touching every curve and hollow like it was a blessed land. She took a step back to kick off her ankle boots. The baggie pants came next. Finally, she rolled away the two pairs of grey leggings. As she hooked her thumbs into the string waistband at her hips, his hoarse choke stopped her. He shook his head and she left the white bikini panties where they were.

"Turn."

She did as he asked, moving in place while he watched with sleepy, hot eyes. She didn't even give him any flack for forgetting to put it in the form of a question. She had better things to do. She made short work of her braid, undoing the plait so the curls would trail down her back. A peek over her shoulder found Travis's uncompromised attention and his white-knuckled grip on the armrests. A girl could spend her whole life hoping to be stared at like that. Vetta tucked the sensation away into her heart, to be remembered later, when he was gone. For now, for tonight, she wanted all of him she could get.

The question was...how much of *her* could he take?

She could hardly call herself a scientist if she didn't try to find out.

Closing her eyes, she twined her hands upward, pulling her hair up with her fingertips. It was soft, she realized, warming to the thought of feeling herself as he might. If she were a man, what would she want to touch?

She turned, curving into her own hands as they smoothed down her throat to her bare breasts. She lifted the warm flesh in each hand. Did he ever notice how much softer the skin was here? Silkier. She lifted them, pressing them together to feel the smooth skin brushing the other breast and heard a masculine groan. He liked that. What else would he like?

She let her fingers separate around the nipples and continued pressing them together, the added friction sending streaks of heat down her belly. Between her thighs, the warmth and the wetness began to build. Her lids parted, and she saw Travis before her, watching her hands like a man under a spell. What would he do if she did this?

Her hand moved, as it had a thousand times in the privacy of her shower, following the tightening of her muscles down her stomach to the elastic of her silk panties. His gaze followed, as hot as ever before, burning the back of her hand as it slipped beneath the fabric to the moist lips below.

She never thought she'd be doing something like this, touching herself in front of Travis Carmichael of all people, and yet, a part of her she never knew existed seemed to blossom to life. Her breath shuddered out of her as her fingertips parted her folds, caressing her clit until she gasped. She closed her eyes again, listening to the sound of his increasingly fast breathing and dipping her fingers inside herself. All at once, she was back in her shower, thinking of him, imagining his hands, his mouth, only this time she knew exactly how all that felt. She whimpered as her flesh pulsed and her own wetness increased. No matter how she touched herself, it would never be what he could offer.

She opened her eyes to see his gaze had gone molten. She pulled her fingers from herself and leaned forward to put them to his lips. He didn't hesitate to take hold of her wrist and open his mouth to taste her. She took her hand away before he could pull her down again. Because she still wanted to taste him.

She bent, keeping her gaze locked on his while using her hands to slither between his open thighs so she could kneel before him. "I can't tell you how many times I've wanted to do this."

His eyes widened. She reached for the button at the top of his fly. He lifted his hips to let her. The sound of his zipper sliding down was the only sound other than her own careful breathing. Beneath the placket, she could feel his erection.

"You've wanted to go down on me?"

"Not exactly." Unfolding the denim, she reached in to take hold of his cock, the thick flesh hot in her palm. "But I have always wanted to get the upper hand with you."

His grin was more a flash of teeth. "You don't say."

She stroked gently, running her fingers up and down the shaft before taking her hands away completely. He growled, but she only shook her head at him. "I want you to get these off."

"But I want you to get *me* off."

"One thing at a time." She licked her lips, just to see if it would motivate him.

His answer was to lean forward and pull off his shirt by the back of his collar and throw it over the side before lying back in the chair like a demigod, waiting to be served. His heavy-lidded gaze all but ate her up, keeping her warm despite the lack of clothes. Feeling more than a little empowered by that, she reached for the waistband of his jeans and began pulling. He lifted his hips and let her strip him, grinning at her when she balled up the pants and tossed them over her shoulder.

As specimens went, one couldn't want for much with Travis Carmichael. She let her senses feast on him, every tawny inch from his head to his toes. Running her palms gently up his legs, she smiled at the tickling of his body hair against her skin. She lowered her face to his thigh, feeling the bristly hairs with her cheek, inhaling the heated scent of him. Soap, something tart but fresh, inviting and mysterious. So very, very different from her own scent. Beneath her touch, he quivered, holding still while she inspected. Finally, or so she gathered from his relieved release of breath, she slid her hands to the thick erection. In their times together so far, she had only gotten to glimpse at it, but even then she'd known he was different than the plastic replicas. It moved in her hand, jumping as she stroked upward and back down. She felt moisture at the tip and wondered what he'd do if she licked it away.

In the books she'd read, men seemed to like that. But literature and real life had never coincided before. Suddenly, the heated sensuality began to fade and she was unsure what to do next.

He'd laid out the rules before. Maybe he'd lay them out again. "Tell me what you want," she made herself say, keeping her eyes trained on his body instead of meeting his gaze. She'd give too much away.

"Look at me," he said gently, slipping his hand into the hair at her temple. "A man wants a woman who wants him. Look me in the eyes when you touch me. I don't fuck martyrs."

She frowned. "I'm not martyring."

"Good. Then touch me like you want me. Show me you're as into it as I am." He cupped his hand around hers to show her the pressure he wanted. "Wrap your hand around it and hold it to your mouth. Just like that. Now wet your lips."

She watched him watching her, pausing to take it all in. He held his breath, waiting for her to give him what he wanted. What he needed. The power of her position went straight to her head. He might have all the experience, but *she* was the one in control now.

He groaned, as if he understood her realization. "Hurry, Vetta."

She folded her bottom lip into her mouth, letting it slip out slow and wet before gliding it across the deep-blush-colored glans. The wide head pulsed, hot and moist, against her. He pushed a breath out through his teeth when she moved her tongue close, just millimeters from touching it...and stopped.

Oh, yes, this could be fun.

She opened her mouth once more, her tongue just nipping beneath the corona, watching Travis for any indication of pleasure. His gaze burned as if fevered and the flush to his cheekbones rose while his jaw tightened. She dipped her head and allowed herself to lave the underside of his cock from the base all the way back to the tip.

His hips bucked suddenly and he swore fiercely. That counted. Pleased with herself, she smiled and did it again. His hand tightened in her hair and he pushed against her, trying to guide her in one direction or another, but she took her time. This was better than ice cream.

"God, Vetta, put it in your mouth already."

"What if I don't want to yet?" She licked all around the head.

Travis gripped her neck, pulling her away. “I *will* get you back for this.”

She met his gaze easily now, pursing her lips over the whole head and pulling off with a soft pop. “I’m counting on it.”

Chapter Eight

"Isn't this what you wanted?" she asked, delivering another of those long, full tongue licks that had him gripping the fake-leather armrests. "You wanted to see me lick up one side..." She tilted her head, using her hand to pull his cock toward herself gently. "And down the other. Remember?"

He thought back on that conversation in her bedroom—was it only yesterday?—and couldn't believe he was ever so stupid. Clearly, his brain hadn't been engaged. If it had been, it would have realized watching her, as he was doing now, he would never last long enough to have each of his fantasies fulfilled.

"You wanted me to suck you deep, remember?" Her silvery stare met his own and she gave a quick wink before guiding him between her lips and the incredible sensation of her sucking on him damn near had *his* eyes rolling up in his head. Her cheeks hollowed in time with the slide of her tongue underneath and around the head. Then she made his day. She began to pump him into her mouth, her hand down below, gripping where she couldn't fit him in. He loved watching her try, though.

She set a slow pace, ignoring the cues he gave her to hurry. As if she recognized somehow that she had all the control. He didn't like that thought. Determined to remind both of them what this affair was about, he grasped the side of her head and tilted her face to look up at him. She let her wet lips come off him only when she was ready.

"I thought you wanted to watch me swallow," she murmured, her face flushed. With passion or power? Either was damn hot, but one was dangerous.

"I want you to turn around."

She did what he ordered, peering over her shoulder as he leaned forward and put his hands on her hips. His thumbs caressed beneath the edges of her white panties. He felt her shiver against his palms. This was more like it. He could keep his perspective, his distance, if he wasn't her willing plaything. Much better when she was his.

His let his thumbs follow the fabric to the lowest curve of her ass, getting a grip and parting the cheeks there. She gasped, jumping a little, but not going away. No, she pushed back into his palms. He rewarded her by pressing his face to the curve and giving it a sucking kiss.

She shuddered, a soft little sob catching in her throat.

His thumbs moved lower again, in between her thighs to find the wetness he was hoping for. She melted with a slight whimper, falling forward even more. No longer interested in playing, Travis hooked the panties with his fingers and pulled them down her legs. Then he gave himself the treat of licking at the plump lips of her pussy as she bent to free her feet of the panties. It wasn't enough. He knew exactly what he wanted now. What he'd wanted for years.

He yanked her down, gathering her against him and guiding himself into her heat.

Putting one hand on her hip and reaching around her slim ribcage, he palmed her breast. Using firm pressure, he began the grinding motion into her. Vetta picked it up quickly, swirling her hips with each rise, twisting them again on the downturn. Soon, he was pumping upward just to prolong the delicious sensation of being inside her.

She moaned, letting her head fall back onto his shoulder. Complete and total surrender. Triumph filled him. He wrapped an arm around her waist, pulling her backward onto him and sending the headrest of the chair backward into its full reclining position so fast it clanked.

"Try something with me," he said, pulling her hair away from her throat so he could taste the sleek muscles of her neck. She nodded, helping him by supporting her weight on her hands, which were now on the armrests of the chair. Carefully, he guided one of her legs over the armrests as well, and she followed suit on the other side. Now she was open, her back arched, ready for him to toy with as he pleased.

Definitely better.

But where to start? He smoothed his hands around the subtle curve of her hips, grazing her belly just to hear her gasp. So many options available. Shifting them upward, he cupped her breast, just barely grazing her nipple. She shook, her pussy tightening around him in reflex. His left hand meandered downward, where her clit, wet and straining, awaited friction. He circled it and she whimpered.

"Will you make noise for me this time, Vetta?"

She answered with a roll of her hips.

He let go of her breast to still her. So she hadn't given up hope of control yet, had she? He swirled the clit again, stopping when she pressed her hips forward to guide his touch.

"Do you want more?"

"More what?"

Using his restraining hand, he braced her and pushed deeper into her. Once. Twice. A third time, just because her creamy peach felt too damn good to stop. Garnering his own control, he took a gentle bite of her shoulder. “More sensation.”

“Couldn’t I just...” She bounced, using her spread legs on the armrests as a base, she rose and sank in quick succession, damn near ending this game before it got anywhere good. He used both hands to hold her still now.

“No, you can’t.”

“But I *want* to.” Every twitch of her hips was like to set him off and she kept twisting in his hold, reveling in her ability to drive him up a goddamn wall. He let her go, watching her shift her weight with her hands, riding him in a smooth rise and fall. She arched her back, taking him deep and kicking up her hips just before lifting up once more. For just a minute, he closed his eyes and let her have her way. Slow, deep, her sighs could have been music. He opened his eyes, watching her move. He didn’t think he’d seen a more beautiful sight. Her hair loose and swaying, her head tilted back, cheeks flushed while she sought out her own pleasure.

In him.

Something in him froze. He shouldn’t be thinking this way. Shouldn’t be looking at her like she was anything more than a good sex partner. And yet, he remained entranced.

That couldn’t be allowed.

He put his hands on her back, circling around to find her breasts. She moaned when he plucked her nipples, the pressure harder than he might have used before. She gasped when he began pumping again, taking over the pace and pushing it to a faster speed. Faster and deeper still. He wanted her surrender.

“Who’s fucking you, Vetta?” he asked roughly. He wanted the moment as raw as possible. Letting go of one nipple, he reached around her for her pussy, slotting her clit between his fingertips while she cried out. “Tell me,” he demanded, letting her stir as she would in response. Damn if he was going to stop her now.

“You are.”

“I am what?”

Finally, she seemed to realize something was going on. She looked over her shoulder, her eyes losing the glaze of pleasure as she focused on his face. He watched her form the words, her lips still wet from sucking on him, but he realized too late she wasn’t playing his game. He stilled as her whole body softened into his arms. She tilted her face toward his, her eyes closed while her hand pulled him into her kiss. A soft, generous kiss. As if she meant to comfort him.

And suddenly he knew which of them was really getting fucked.

He didn’t want to feel anything soft and sweet. He wanted raw, hard sex that didn’t have anything to do with the respect he saw in her eyes earlier. Or the succor she offered now as her body began to undulate slowly over him. He wanted to tell her to stop. Wanted to prop her up and pound himself into her until all they had was oblivion. Instead, he kissed her back. He moved with her, twining his arms around her and holding her close.

It wasn’t what he wanted, but the intimacy was exactly what he needed. Her warmth. Her passion. She gave it too freely. He couldn’t have pushed it away to save his life. And when she gave a keening cry, her body so tight around him as he came, he knew things had officially spun out of control.

Afterward, she curled up on his lap, still catching her breath as she fell asleep, the smallest moan escaping her as she snuggled her face beneath his jaw. He felt his own heartbeat starting to slow, even as a sense of panic began to fill him again.

Caring about Vetta was one thing, and that was already too big of a thing, but this feeling he had now...it was wrong. It shouldn't be happening. It shouldn't fucking be happening.

He wanted to be angry. Not at her so much as at himself. But he couldn't muster it up. He'd gotten himself into this mess. If he'd had any kind of control, she wouldn't be under his skin in the first place. But he'd allowed himself a moment of weakness and gave in to temptation. Over and over again. If he'd been smart, he'd have run out on her when Jade showed up with her pan of eggs. A braining with a hot iron pot might have done him some good.

Now he was stuck with the outcome he wanted the least: wishing things could be different. Wishing there were a way he could stay, could have this...have *her*.

He felt around on the floor for something to cover her with. He usually kept a blanket nearby but hell if he could see it anywhere. Finally, his fingers met the collar of his shirt, so he plucked it off the ground and carefully draped it over her. If his heart surged when she sighed against him, he couldn't let himself think about it. He couldn't think about anything but finding solid ground again. Worrying about how it would feel to lose her wouldn't make it any easier. Besides, he already knew how to live with regrets.

Vetta woke up slow. Loathe to open her eyes, she cuddled into a warm, hard pillow, surprised at the smooth silken heat under her cheek. Her eyes opened without permission and she realized the pillow wasn't a pillow, it was Travis. The soft fuzzy blanket was his big flannel shirt from the night before. And that hard, restraining bar anchoring her was his arm, his fingers splayed around the curve of her hip. She looked around the unfamiliar room, trying to shake the equally unfamiliar sleep cobwebs away. Slowly, images of the night before replayed in her mind. Touching Travis, kissing...riding...thrusting...

"Anyone ever tell you that you wake up just like a cat?"

Vetta jumped, clutching his shirt to her chest automatically. Travis peered up at her, looking as misty as she felt.

She cleared her throat before attempting to talk. "No, usually I'm compared to the undead. I just open my eyes and get to whatever I was thinking about. Apparently, it's creepy," she added, rubbing her cheek at the obscure memory.

"Let me guess...your mother told you that."

She blinked at his insight. "How did you know?"

"It's not a shock." She watching him pick up a lock of her hair and flip the ends over her shoulder. "Svetlana is the only person I've ever known who is frightened by the prospect of waking up and thinking."

Vetta smirked rather than laugh. If only she could argue. "To think, she only says nice things about you." Usually things like, "If he were only a few years younger..."

"Hey, you know I like your mother." That was an understatement. He and Svetlana got on like a house on fire. Svetlana always made time to visit with Travis whenever she showed up, something that sprung a nerve Vetta didn't like to admit she had. He even got along with Penny, whenever her father managed to show up at her lab. She wasn't really surprised. The only person on Earth he didn't get along with was her. Well, her and whatever annoying man was trying to bilk her at any given time. Given his views on living off women, she finally had a reason for that particular idiosyncrasy.

Travis seemed to be thinking about her parents too, because he shook his head and broke through her thought processes. “If you didn’t look so much like Svetlana, I’d swear you were adopted.”

She laughed, leaning her head back on his shoulder, surprised at how comfortable it was to lay skin to skin against him. “I had the DNA run once, just to check. I really only needed to do some basic research on my family. It turns out *Penny* is the anomaly. Most of his ancestors were entrepreneurs and inventors. Not a single playboy in more than six generations.”

“That’s where the money comes from, then?”

“Patents,” she agreed with a sigh. Normally a question like that would have her antennae tingling. But this was *Travis*. “God alone knows how he ended up with my mother.” For all his good qualities, Vetta knew Penny wasn’t a lady-killer thanks to his charm or good looks, which didn’t exist. Penny strolled around in a state of perpetual boredom, which often made him less tactful than even herself. He wasn’t particularly handsome or tall, and sometimes you had to wonder if he knew you were in the same room with him. But he was kind-hearted, generous and her mother always claimed he could make her laugh. Lots of women seemed to share the opinion. Vetta had yet to see him alone, even after her mother had left him.

“Right place, right time, I guess,” Travis said, sounding amused, but not particularly interested. He’d been dragging that lock of her hair over her shoulder.

“More like right yacht, wrong country,” Vetta scoffed, wondering where he’d take his little paintbrush next. “The way I hear it, Penny thought he was in Monte Carlo. Apparently, he’d docked in Cannes and the rest was history.” A lame, excuse-filled history.

"Only your father could make international travel sound like a wrong turn."

"Count yourself lucky you didn't grow up with him. My entire childhood was a series of wrong turns. Between him and Svetlana, I've probably been left in every English-speaking country there is." Once the words were out, Vetta realized how they sounded. Ungrateful. As if she were making a bid for pity. She knew good and well that Travis was the last person who'd ever pity her. "Once Jade was with me, getting left behind was sort of the plan."

"And now?"

She frowned.

"You know. What's your plan now? Does it include your parents?"

"Well, I haven't given it much thought." Hardly any at all. What was there to plan? She'd keep herself occupied, keep an eye on her parents' financial matters and take care of Jade. But did she have plans to include them on her decisions or plans for the future? Not even if they stayed in one place long enough. "They have their lives, I have mine. We see each other when we can. Not much different than most families." She turned away from the almost confused look on his face. "Not everyone has what you had with your mother, Travis. Not even most people. Believe me when I say you were lucky."

"I know," he murmured and she felt what could almost be a soothing motion from his hand on her hip. Suddenly, sitting naked under a shirt comparing families seemed utterly ridiculous. This definitely didn't fall under the heading of uncomplicated sex.

"I should get going. Jade's already up." She sat up, preparing to hop off the recliner when a sharp jolt went up her spine. Both of them froze. “Was that my back or the chair?”

“Could have been both.”

Gingerly, she uncurled her legs and alighted. Her body was sore, but nothing else registered a noise of complaint. The recliner, on the other hand, wasn’t so forgiving. As soon as she stood, it slumped to the left side, thumping the concrete and putting Travis at a hard tilt.

Vetta held the shirt up and waited for the recliner to crumble. It made a creaking noise, but that was it.

“Could I make a suggestion?” she asked carefully, watching his face for the dark scowl to lift.

“Does it involve dollar signs?”

“Not directly, no.”

He growled. Or maybe it was a sigh. *Note number eighty-six: Men use sounds instead of words when acting in a grudging manner. Perhaps this is to enable them to claim they didn’t expressly give an answer?*

“I’m thinking that I’d like to add some furnishings to the apartment here, to increase the rental value,” she tacked on in a hurry when he pinned her with a glare that could have split atoms. She concentrated on fitting her arms into the sleeves of his shirt and tugging it closed around her.

“No.”

“Travis—”

“I said no.”

“We can’t sleep on that chair again. It’ll probably finish breaking when you stand up.”

“Then we’ll sleep on the floor.”

That made her laugh. Until she realized he was serious. “You’re out of your mind.”

"So you've told me." Which meant he wasn't budging.

Yet.

"Let me see if I have this right." She started counting on her fingers. "There's a perfectly good bed in my apartment, which you won't use because you're afraid of Jade."

"I'm not afraid—"

Second finger. "And you won't let me buy a bed to keep over here because you think that's living off me."

"No, I think it's a waste of—"

"And now you actually think I'm going to come over here and have sex on a concrete floor, just because you said so. Do I have my facts straight?"

It took him a second before he grunted an admission.

"Good. Now I'm going to give you a few facts. First one, I'm rich."

"Believe me, I know that one."

She wagged the second finger on her other hand at him. "I also have standards. Such as, I will sell you on the street corner before *I* sleep on concrete."

"And third?" he asked, probably because he was trying not to kill her.

"No bed. No sex."

He sputtered, the jerk. "That's not a fact. We barely used the bed when we had it."

She crossed her arms. "It's a fact now. I'm not spending the next several weeks wallowing on the ground like a pig. You're the deviant around here, not me."

"Does the fact that I don't want this register at all in your oversize brain?" he demanded, tone sour and if she didn't miss her guess, petulant. Meaning he was running out of excuses.

"It never has before. I don't see why I should start now."

He rolled his eyes, shifting his weight in the chair, which clunked unevenly backward. Vetta raised her eyebrow. He ignored her. "And you wonder why I never get involved with women."

"I hadn't noticed you switching to men."

He scrubbed his eyes wearily. "I'm not hearing this."

"Good. Then we're decided. I'm buying a bed."

"Damn it, Vetta."

"Expect a delivery by this afternoon." She started picking up her clothes from next to the chair, careful to stay out of reach this time. He probably could have gotten her, but she'd bet his pride demanded that he not risk the chair collapsing in front of her.

Note number eight-seven: Men will do just about anything not to look stupid. Including act *stupid.*

She blew him a kiss and winked. Then she got out before he thought better of it and throttled her. Her sense of triumph lasted all of the five minutes it took her to get dressed and get back to her own apartment area.

Jade was, to say the least, unhappy.

While Vetta showered, Jade had knocked her knuckles blue on the door demanding to know when the wedding was taking place. Vetta hummed to drown out the sound and told herself she was happy with the situation as it was. And she was. She was getting exactly what she wanted without any false expectations. Not to mention she was getting all kinds of insight into how men thought. That right there was priceless.

Not that any of them were going to make sense anytime soon, but they didn't strike her as money-hungry penises with legs anymore. Ironic, since most of her time with Travis was spent panting like an asthmatic. As much fun as that was, she found herself musing most over the things she learned from him when he wasn't on top of her. The way he put actual thought into conversing with her. She'd always known he was a proud man, but it was refreshing to realize he was idealistic. His drive had always impressed her, but now that she knew his reasons for working so hard, she found herself respecting him. Yes, he was aggravating. But he was also gentle. Kind. He'd held her close last night, drifting off with a warm sigh into her hair. She'd like to imagine he might have been taking one last deep breath of her before he relaxed for a few hours. Stupid and fantastical, yes, but the romantic part of her—the part she'd thought died somewhere around Svetlana's third marriage—wagged its tail at the completely insupportable theory.

He might be sleeping with her for the sex and only the sex, but it was nice to come to the conclusion that the man she was having her first affair with was also a man she liked. Liked a lot.

"Fine," Jade snapped through the door. "But don't think you duckin' nothin', little girl. If the two of you don't come to dinner tonight, I promise you, you *will* be sorry."

Vetta wrapped herself in a towel and laughed. Jade had made similar vows of extreme retribution when Vetta refused to sleep as a child.

"I'll call your parents."

Vetta froze.

"You think I'm mad, your mother'll have your hide."

That was an understatement. For all her sophistication, there was a reason Svetlana had been married nine times. She had a hard time separating sex from love. And Penny. Oy. He wouldn't care about the affair. He'd just think it was his fatherly job to interrogate Travis and prove him financially unworthy of marrying her. This was Penny, after all. By the time anyone got him to realize they weren't getting married, the humiliating would be done.

"You wouldn't," Vetta said, staring at the door, too stunned to open it. It had always been her and Jade against the world—a world inhabited by Penny and Svetlana, in particular. One little affair and Jade was switching sides?

"You wanna bet?"

No, not really. Jade and scruples had parted ways decades ago.

"You know what? I want you both here for dinner *every* night from now on."

Vetta pulled the door open. "You can't be serious."

Jade's frown could only be called mulish. Her arms were crossed and her lips were pressed hard enough together to mint coins.

"Jade—"

"I didn't raise you to be no man's plaything."

Vetta felt her cheeks flush and she looked down at her hands.

Jade's tone softened when she sighed. "You don't even realize what you're doing, do you? You think you're acting like everyone else, but you're *not* everyone else. You never have been, baby."

Didn't she know it. "You're making more of this relationship than there is. I'm not looking to get married."

"No, you're looking to get loved."

Vetta stepped back, meeting Jade's eyes easily. "No, I'm not. I knew this...fling wasn't about falling in love with anyone."

"I didn't say nothing about *fallin'*." Jade shook her head and walked away. "Dinner's at six as usual."

Vetta closed the door and hoped the shaking she felt had nothing to do with the truth.

Thankfully, Travis agreed to dinner. It wasn't easy, given the king-size bed she ordered arrived at his door at four in the afternoon. Vetta offered him the compromise of keeping it in the lab portion he wasn't using instead of in his living area. He took it when she offered to put it together naked.

She never did get that far because he was too interested in getting her clothes off to concern himself with doing more than throwing the mattress flat on the concrete and having his way with her. Getting him to dinner was more of a challenge. She had to promise all kinds of things he didn't want to wait for. Midway through the meal, Vetta finally had an idea of why Jade wanted them there. She turned every strand of conversation toward marriage with the subtlety of a sledgehammer. By dinner's end, all the blame had formed a target on Vetta's own forehead.

Travis's expression promised revenge.

Jade's promised all-out war.

Vetta gulped her water and wondered which of them was going to do her in first.

Chapter Nine

A month. That was all the time it took for Vetta to decide she should have just let Jade call in Svetlana.

So far, she'd received The Evil Eye about twelve hundred times, countless disks disappeared, Jade's drink—unfortunately bobbled by one of the lab techs while they tried to pass one another—slipped from her hand above the monitor vents of Vetta's main computer, causing the thing to pop, fizz, smoke and join the great Abacus in the sky. The *coup de grace*, however, was the morning Vetta came down to find all their still-to-be-entered applications in neat piles of page one, page two, page three and page four. Since they'd been previously stapled together in sets of applicant, it reeked of sabotage. If each page hadn't been stamped with registration numbers prior to use, the entire lot would have had to be exempted from the study. Instead, it was delayed while each applicant page was matched to its corresponding registration number.

What should have been a week of entering information turned into two weeks of deflecting crises. And yet, none of them seemed to matter all that much. The driving need to get the experiment completed had faded into a need not to let it end. It didn't make sense, but she just knew, down in her bones, that if the experiment came to an end, her time with Travis would, too. Jade's antics didn't even upset her because the entire building seemed in a type of daze, with very little changing and almost nothing important being discussed. Day after day, Vetta worked on entering information, making notes on her laptop about Travis or undoing Jade's handiwork, until dinner. Sometimes Vetta ate with them, sometimes she just watched Travis and Jade bicker and tease over thinly veiled references to getting married, but her day didn't really begin until she and Travis would cross together to Travis's lab bed and spend the night pretending another day hadn't passed.

Vetta got good at ignoring other truths. Truths like occasionally catching Jade watching her sadly whenever she forgot to be angry. It would make her wonder why Jade was so sad...and she'd figure it out in 2.6 seconds, leaving too big a knot in her stomach to deal with. So, she ignored it. Just like the boxes starting to show up a little less sporadically in Travis's lab or the look he'd have on his face when the mailbox delivered nothing but air.

She was the model of a supportive female, asking him if he needed any research help finding other groups studying his field, or even a reference for his new landlord; whomever that might be. She even assigned one of her techs to stuffing his resume envelopes when he left the pile on his lab table one night. She made a few rough stabs at offering him a grant again, right along with offering to help resell his more delicate and expensive instruments, but all offers were politely turned down.

Travis turned down everything she offered, with exception to her body and her time. It went without saying he wouldn't accept her heart, either. It was the one thing she was smart enough not to put on the table.

For his part, Travis didn't find any immediate positions in San Diego but he did seem to catch more than his share of Jade's wrath. When he expressed an interest in looking up local storage, the phone books in both their labs mysteriously disappeared. But he made sure not to mention he could still find what he needed off the Internet. God only knew what Jade would have done to his computer. The pile of boxes that he'd stored in the hall as he unloaded his old truck's flatbed were miraculously leaked on by enough water to down the Titanic. He'd managed to put an ad in the local paper to sell the truck only to find that it suddenly didn't run thanks to a missing carburetor. She'd checked high and low in the building for some sign of the engine part but if Jade were behind the theft, she certainly hadn't left any tracks. What Vetta found instead were stacks of mail that had Travis's name on them, most of it junk, in a plastic crate in Jade's closet. The few pieces of importance were all rejections. Much as she hated to, she gave them to him along with the primary mail key Jade had in her desk.

Vetta wanted to get angry at her, but it didn't take a genius to see that all Jade's tricks were designed to keep Travis there longer. Jade just didn't understand. Keeping him there wouldn't make him belong there. He wouldn't want to *be* there. He wouldn't even be with Vetta if he weren't sure he was leaving. Prolonging the inevitable only made him feel trapped and indebted. Sex could only salve the stress so much. Sooner or later, he'd go and Jade was just going to have to accept it. And so would she.

Shaking out of her almost-misery, Vetta concentrated on the laptop in front of her. She'd brought it over to make notes while Travis slept, tucking it underneath the bed frame when she wasn't using it. In front of her was the collection of notes she'd made over the weeks that even she couldn't delude herself into thinking were about anything more than holding onto Travis in some way or another. She and Jade didn't have very different goals after all.

#859: He's so warm when he sleeps. And his face seems almost young when he's relaxed. Not as jaded. There's a scent from his throat I cannot identify, but it's comforting. Pheromones?

#860: X-Position notes: He seems to enjoy this one. I think it has something to do with being able to see his effect on me, as he's equally prone to other front-facing positions. He's made references to wishing we had a mirror wall. Responds best to visual stimulus combined with verbal challenge. It's not enough to use profanity. It's almost as if he likes to vie for control.

#861: Have checked online sources for facing positions to test theory...

"Montana!" Travis's voice, excited like she hadn't heard in a while, echoed from the other side of the lab, where the stairwell door from his apartment opened.

Vetta jumped, nearly unbalancing the lightweight computer off her lap. She quickly folded it and tucked it back into the space beneath the support beam, watching him bound across the open room with a smile on his face and a paper in his hand. She only had enough time to find her feet and rise before he whisked her right back off them, spinning her in a circle and whooping like a madman.

"I just got a fax from Dr. Donaldson. Remember him? He was—"

"Our Cellular Development professor," Vetta said, looking up at his flushed face. He *was* excited. Thrilled, really. Her fingers tightened on his sleeves against her will. He was leaving. And he was happy about it.

To stave the panic, she forced her mind to work. "He-he published some studies on female hormones a few months ago."

"Yes and he's making some real progress. He was something of a mentor to me," he added, his voice softening as he explained.

She knew that, of course. Dr. Donaldson and Travis often had their heads together after sessions. Donaldson's was the one class where the teacher, though always polite, was firmly entrenched on Travis's side. She'd even gotten a B on a paper from him. Donaldson would never settle for mediocre from anyone, even when her mediocre was someone else's Nobel Prize. She'd rather liked the man. *Then.*

"I e-mailed him, on the off chance he might need some extra hands. He's been away at a conference in New York without access, said he just got back and didn't even unpack before responding. He's offered me a position as his second. He wants me to come as soon as I can."

Travis finally took a breath, his expectant expression a little too much for Vetta to handle right then. She blinked, the annoying sting of tears causing a lump the size of Jade's famous biscuits to form in her throat. She couldn't say a thing, not that she knew what to say anyway.

Congratulations?

I'm happy for you?

Don't leave me?

"Vetta?" Finally, it seemed to dawn on him that she wasn't going to be happy about this. His smile melted away, his hands dropped a few inches on her back to her hips. He finally noticed her panicked hold on him.

She released him, smoothing the creases she probably made in his gray flannel shirt with a pat. She cleared her throat, swallowing any urge to cry. She wouldn't cry in front of him, wouldn't make him feel bad when she'd gone to such pains to get herself into this situation. She pasted her best paparazzi smile on her face, but had a feeling it didn't reach her eyes. "So, when do you go?"

"I told him I'd be there by Thursday." His eyes darkened and she felt horrible for stealing that light from him. He was the one who had faced the fear of not having anywhere to go, the one who worried about his next meal. She'd never had that worry in her life. She had no right to take his relief from him.

"That gives us time to celebrate!" Even to her, her voice was bright enough to break glass.

"Vetta—"

"No, no arguing this time. We're going to dinner and I'm buying. Call it my goodbye gift."

His mouth tightened, probably from the urge to say something she didn't want to hear. He let his hands fall and Vetta stepped back from him. *Retreat and regroup, retreat and regroup...*

"I have to go...upstairs." Lame, she knew, but her imagination deserted her. "Six o'clock okay? Dress nice, I know just the place. Svetlana's always raving about it."

Travis only nodded. Vetta took that as permission to flee, so she did. Upstairs, away, where she found her tears couldn't be held back anymore.

Later, she lay in her bed hoping the worst of her crying was over. She had no right to be crying. Her heart had no right to hurt this way. Rationally, she'd always known he would leave. That was always his plan and he'd never shown any sign he had an inclination to change it. So why did she feel as if he were doing something horrible?

She wiped at her moist temples, wishing the tears would stop slipping down that same path into her hair. Her sleeve was getting soaked and it wasn't stopping half of them.

"Tissue?"

Vetta didn't bother looking to her side where Jade had

inexplicably materialized to sit on her bedside chair. “You practice sneaking up on people, don’t you?” she complained as she rolled onto her back.

“I’d do better at it if we didn’t have so many stairs, but you were snifflin’ too hard to hear me and my brass band anyway.”

Vetta rubbed at her eyes again, rougher this time. Her chest ached and the sobbing started again and the words bubbled out of her. “He’s leaving for sure now.”

“He was leavin’ for sure before.”

She turned her head to glare at her nanny. “You being logical isn’t helping, Jade.”

“Won’t do no good, both of us movin’ to Egypt. Denial might have a pretty view, but I’ve found the return trip’s a lot nastier than getting there.”

“I am not in denial,” Vetta said carefully, accepting the proffered tissue and folding it in her fingers. Precise corner to precise corner. “I’m not. I knew what I was doing getting involved with him. I knew he was leaving. I accepted that. I just didn’t know when. Now I do and it’s sooner than I expected, that’s all. I wanted longer to say goodbye.”

“Most people call what you two been up to *hello*.”

“Well, not us,” she snapped, sitting up and throwing her legs over the side of the bed. She shrugged out of her lab coat and threw it in the general direction of the hamper. She missed by a foot and a half.

“Funny how what looks so simple can be so hard, eh?”

Vetta ripped her gaze from the coat. “I gave my word that I wouldn’t try to hold onto him,” she said, reminding herself as much as Jade. “He deserves this chance to work with his mentor. He deserves to keep his promise to his mother, to not have to worry about the rest of his life.”

"He *deserves* to have someone love him," Jade added quietly. "And so do you."

Vetta shook her head. "I have people who love me. Travis has no one."

"He has *you.*" Jade's brow furrowed with emphasis.

But the words didn't bring her the epiphany that Jade so obviously expected. They only brought the painful truth up in stark relief.

"That's just it, Jade." Her heart felt like it was caving in. "He doesn't *want* me."

Before Jade could raise any arguments, Vetta pulled her bath towel off the hook behind her door and went to take a shower. She had a dinner date to prepare for.

Vetta did an almost-decent imitation of being happy for him, but Travis could happily kick himself a few thousand times for making her gray-green eyes well up, causing that stricken stillness to her face. He should have realized how she'd take his news. Should have been gentler. But no, he'd been so excited, so goddamned *relieved* to finally be able to breathe that all he could think about was sharing it with her. In the process, he'd all but blindsided her with what amounted to an eager announcement that he was ending their arrangement.

Sitting on the bed where he'd committed the near-fatal error of growing accustomed to sleeping warm and comfortable, Travis held his head in his hands and asked himself one more time what the hell he'd gotten himself into. This was not an arrangement and he knew it. At the least, it wasn't the arrangement he'd expected. He should have stuck to his usual fuck-'em-and-duck-'em game plan the second he realized he was getting in too deep. The women he was with were usually of the same mind. He never worried about them afterward and they never worried about him. This was too complicated to be an arrangement.

As for getting in too deep, a good twenty minutes of brooding made him admit he'd been in too deep from the beginning. The problem was deciding when the beginning was. Did it start when he moved in with her? Or was it only when he allowed himself to touch her? Much as he hated to admit it to himself, she'd been dangerous from the second he met her, simply because he liked her so much. She'd caught his attention at first glance. When he hadn't been able to get her out of his mind, he'd turned her into an enemy. Kept her at arm's length at every turn because he'd known she was someone who might actually mean something to him, if he let himself. And yet, he hadn't been able to ignore her. Not back in school, not after he moved into her building and sure as hell not now, when she'd offered him everything he thought he ever wanted from her.

A month in her bed and he still didn't have enough of her. Not her scent. Not her body. Not her evil little grin or the sound of her laughter as it echoed off the walls of the lab in the middle of the night.

No, this was no damn *arrangement.*

It was a disaster.

And in three days, it would end.

He lay back across the width of the mattress, staring up at the ceiling, waiting for the heavy viselike grip on his chest to ease. Three days and a lifetime with Vetta was over. It felt unfair. Unbelievable. Wrong. How could a month have made so much of a difference in his entire life?

Had giving in to his hunger for her somehow changed everything he'd done to make her hate him for the last seven years into some kind of deranged love note? Because it felt like it.

Unwillingly, he remembered his mother's death. Losing her had made him feel completely alone in the world. Vetta had connected him when nothing and no one else could. She alone got him through those last months of his education with her prodding and challenges, though it took him a long time to realize how much gentler she'd been about it than usual. Had she known how much he needed her to motivate him?

Her family all but adopted him after he'd moved in, from zany Svetlana and her always-belated birthday balloons, thick accent and breezy visits when she'd act as if she'd been gone mere hours instead of months, to the occasionally featherbrained Penny, who assumed Travis had married Vetta when he came by during Travis's move in and had not been dissuaded of this opinion ever since. No doubt, poor Penny would take a few years to decide he and Vetta had "divorced" and Vetta's only recourse would be to admit, yes, they had, just to end the discussion.

Lord only knew what Penny would do then. As it was, whenever they saw each other, Penny was prone to ask when Travis would be taking over the chief scientific officer's position in his megalomaniacal pharmaceutical company. Even Jade, whom he always sensed got as much enjoyment out of his sparring with Vetta as the two of them did, had always had a smile and a wink for him. These days, even upset with him as she was, she also tended to have a snack for him as well.

In three days, all that would be gone too.

Travis had the feeling that the loneliness he'd felt in his mother's absence might just pale compared to losing the St. Claire family en masse. It definitely would to losing Vetta, all by herself. He couldn't believe it, but in his not-as-hard-as-he-thought heart, it was true.

This last month had been the most amazing month of his life. Her smiles were all for him, for the first time ever, with nothing held back. Her impish humor was shared with him instead of smeared all over him. Every night, they ate dinner, cleaned up and teased Jade about her addiction to sitcoms and gruesome police dramas. Then, they'd lose themselves in each other's arms until the night ran out.

One month and—despite Jade's constant sabotage—they were all as cozy as if they'd been together this way for years. If he didn't think about what they *didn't* say, it would be the perfect memory.

But he did think about it, in the hours he spent alone while he packed his lab up. How Vetta would rather sleep in the colder lab bed than sleep in her own, with or without him. How she bit her lip whenever she asked about his job search, leaving it nearly punctured when she carefully sighed in relief that he'd heard nothing. He didn't doubt her sincerity when it came to her desire to see him secure. She'd offered grants herself, half teasingly, that she always graciously nodded and shrugged at when he'd decline in the same vein. They never said how serious they both knew the other was. And now they'd never say how they felt about each other.

He wasn't an idiot, it would hurt her to think that she'd given him everything and he didn't care, but it was better than thinking they could make it work long distance. She'd always need to be here in San Diego. The only home that had ever been stable was the one she made for herself in that lab. Her parents needed her, that much was obvious. She was the center they built their tangented lives from. And he...he was married to his work.

If he were actually on a usual schedule, whole days would frequently go by without his thinking about her even once, or having spent any time with her. When he went to bed at night it was usually to sleep in an exhausted heap, not to make love until sunrise spilled through his windows.

Vetta deserved someone who could commit to her first, the way her family never had. The way he never could. Whomever she found someday, that person would never be him.

All he'd have with her was tonight.

It would have to last him forever.

Chapter Ten

The restaurant was the kind of place she shunned normally. It was exclusive, classically designed in dark woods and fine linens, crystal tastefully dripping from every visible surface, carpet so thick you could drop the finest china on it without so much as a chip or a thump. Every table managed to be an intimate nook, lit with glowing candles floating in bowls of sparkling water.

Guiding Vetta with a hand to her bare spine, Travis could tell exactly what she thought of the place: Hell on Earth. He could feel the terror in her, right down to the fine vibration running through her muscles. Not that she had anything to worry about. If anyone did happen to look up from their own intimate dinners, all they would do was stare at her in awe.

Vetta casual, even under all her clothes, could make your gut tighten just by licking her lips as she prepared to call you a name. Tonight, wearing a dress the same color of the inside of a conch shell, its gauzy material fluttering with each step, she was a goddess among mortals. The skirt whispered around her thighs, allowing him to see hints of the shape and shadow in places he wanted to touch and taste, but still protecting her modesty. The upper portion clung to her ribs and breasts before inching to tie behind her neck, leaving her back bare beneath the rippling lengths of her hair. This was a woman who had just come from her lover's bed...or was on her way there soon.

He'd seen her when he'd come to her apartment and nearly dragged her back across the hall to the bed. Her eyes were dramatic, the unexpected eyeliner turning her eyes intense for reasons that had nothing to do with her intellect. Worse, she wore some kind of shiny, wet-looking lipstick that had him halfway aroused all by itself.

And he was the man who got to walk next to her.

For tonight, anyway.

They were seated and her eyes flicked nervously from one corner of the room to the other, her teeth sunk thoughtfully into the plump flesh of her bottom lip.

"I didn't see a single camera when we walked through," he whispered to her.

A relieved expression brought some color to her face. "It's been so long since I've been out dressed this way. Before you came, Jade took pictures. She said my parents wouldn't believe her if she didn't." There it was, that impish grin, giving him the sense that maybe she was relaxing.

"I'm glad she did. You look beautiful."

She fidgeted a little with her skirt, then nodded. "Thank you."

She didn't mean it, it was just the polite thing to say. The same way this fancy dinner was the polite thing to do. A formal goodbye. Something you did for a friend who'd just had a good fortune. He couldn't say why it bothered him that she insisted so hard on it. On ending their time together as friends. It should have been a relief. But it wasn't.

"Can I offer you something from the wine list?" a waiter—who'd materialized out of thin air next to the table—asked, making them both jump.

Vetta shot a look to him he couldn't remember seeing before; utter confusion.

He turned to the waiter. "Another minute, please."

"But of course." The man bowed and disappeared into the shadows.

"What's wrong?"

"Do you know anything about wines?"

"Not really." He shrugged. The most he ever drank was a beer from time to time.

"My mother kept trying to teach me, but I've never really gotten it. There's some sort of trick to it, but I've never had the taste buds to really tell the difference. I know it's supposed to balance your meal or something. Or does it clean your tongue?" She brooded a bit more, looking more herself with a frown of thought. Most of Svetlana's lessons seeped from Vetta's powerful mind like water over a smooth stone, much like the unending list of husbands. Loving her mother was one thing, listening to her was quite another.

"You've drunk champagne at your parents' parties, right?"

Vetta shrugged and nodded.

"Did you like that?"

"The bubbles tickled, but with some sugar cubes, it wasn't too bad."

As if the table were bugged, the waiter returned.

"We'd like a bottle of champagne," Travis heard himself saying as if it were something he asked for regularly. Maybe the night was a game of dress-up for both of them.

"Excellent. Which brand? We have quite a selection." The waiter allowed some pride to seep into his voice as he began listing winemakers and years. The list kept going and after two minutes, Travis realized it was his turn to panic. He looked to

Vetta, who blinked back for a few seconds equally lost. Then, suddenly, she turned to the server with enough sex in her eyes to make *him* start to sweat.

"How about you surprise us with your very best. Money," she assured in her husky tone, "is no object."

"Very good, miss." The waiter bowed and did his disappearing act again.

Vetta dropped the pretense, hitched a shoulder and sighed. "Well, it was worth a shot."

He, on the other hand, needed another second or two to remember how to breathe without putting too much pressure on his inseam. "When the hell did you learn to do that?"

"Do what?"

"Seduce the waiter?"

She actually laughed. "My mother did that to Sean Connery in one of their movies. I copy her whenever I get stuck with people. Worked better for her, though. *He'll* probably bring us Kool-Aid."

The waiter instead arrived with two assistants, a lot of officious fanfare, a standing silver cistern full of ice and a black bottle of Dom Perignon. Travis raised an eyebrow at Vetta. She just raised one back as if this was nothing impressive.

"Let me guess. This is what you always drink."

"It's the kind Svetlana insists on."

Maybe he should get her some Kool-Aid, just for a taste of the exotic. If he were staying, maybe...

The cork was expertly popped, the bottle placed lovingly in the cistern and the assistants vaporized. Then the man began his list of the evening's specials. Travis had an itch to laugh. To him, a special was the cheap item of the hour. To this guy, the special was the rare thing the chef might be convinced to make for you if you paid him enough. The vast differences between his world and Vetta's would have troubled him if Vetta wasn't making unconscious expressions of disgust at the described selections. When the waiter began waning eloquent on filleted snails, Travis knew it was time to call a halt.

"How about you find us some big pieces of cow, grill them just past mooing and you can put anything else on the plate you think should go there. Just don't tell us what it is, okay?" He realized he just didn't have it in him to surprise the man when the waiter simply nodded as if this were how everyone else ordered.

"And some French fries with ketchup, please," Vetta added. "As an appetizer, if you don't mind."

The waiter stumbled at her words. "French fries... Yes, miss."

Okay, so Vetta had it in her.

"By the time we leave here, that guy is going to need retirement."

She narrowed her eyes at him. "Are you saying I'm demanding?"

No, you've never once asked for enough...

"Svetlana would be proud." He smiled at her, knowing that to say anything else would take her right back to that nervous edge.

She nodded her thanks, then raised her water glass. "Here's to the art of driving service people out of their minds. May they never pee in our soups."

Thankfully, he hadn't brought the water glass to his lips yet and only spilled a glop on the snowy tablecloth instead of spraying it in her face.

"So," she said brightly, squaring her shoulders and

becoming all business. "Tell me more about Montana."

He wished he could dredge up as much enthusiasm, but right now, the best he could scrape together was a wan smile. "It snows there."

"Travis."

"We don't have to talk about it now, Vetts. It's our last—" He stopped himself, but already her smile turned brittle. He started to backtrack, but she waved him off.

"We both knew what was going to happen. Let's not lie to each other and pretend either of us believed tonight was anything but the end," she said quietly. She managed to look composed, but he made the mistake of noticing her hand mangling the fine linen napkin next to her plate.

The guilt he'd been supplanting surged into him with all the energy it had been saving since he'd first shut it down. He reached across the table, capturing that tight hand. "I never meant to hurt you, Vetts."

"I know and you're not trying to now. We made a deal." Her smile was forced, her mouth hard and nearly white at the edges. "We can be adults about it. That's what all the women I interviewed for my project said was the best thing to do. They even have special universal remarks, like...it was fun while it lasted. Or we can still be friends. It's not you, it's me. I'll call you. I think there was another one, but I can't remember it now."

Travis took in the shine of her eyes, the rigidity of her body, the freezing temperature of her hand beneath his and the quivering smile she was working so damn hard to keep up and knew he had to play along. This was no place for being honest, not with so many eyes, not when she'd tried so hard to do the right thing for him.

"Probably something like, 'You suck, I hate you, go die'."

Gratitude flickered on her face before she shook her head. "You've never had a woman say that to you and you know it."

He smiled, remembering that she'd said far worse to him herself over the years. "Of course I did. But usually only from the stupid ones."

That wrought a good solid laugh out of her. "And there were plenty of those. What did the smart ones say?"

"I wish things were different," he replied, honesty sneaking in as he remembered goodbyes that never meant much. He looked her in the eyes, already feeling a goodbye that had yet to be said and hurt too damn much to consider. "I wish we could have made this work. I wish loving you was as easy as it was supposed to be. I just...wish."

She didn't cry exactly. Her eyes filled with tears, glittering brighter than the candlelit crystals around them. Pain swept her features, battling her poise, nearly overcoming her as a tear overbalanced and sped off her lashes, dropping so fast he almost didn't see it. She swiped at it, possibly an afterthought for her make-up. He wasn't really sure. Only that the simple gesture was so natural, so Vetta, it broke his heart.

"I wanted to be happy for you," she whispered. "I-I wanted..." She looked up at the ceiling, a careful, shuddering breath easing between her pursed lips. "I thought I could...that *we* could..."

Screw the decorum of the place. He shifted his chair until he was next to her, taking her hands in his and laying his forehead against hers. Her shoulders hitched, her poise slipping away the second he touched her because more than pride, she needed to be sheltered. Were anyone looking, they'd think they were seeing a romantic embrace. They'd never know she had fallen completely apart.

"You've always been in my life," she said, voice breaking,

her hands gripping his tight enough to hurt. "*My* life. You're the only person I've ever known who was with me for me. Just for *me*. Even when we were fighting, you were mine. I don't know what I'm going to do without you."

He let go of her hands to cup her face and hold her away a few inches. A few more tears had seeped past her guard and he used his thumbs to wipe them away. "You're going to do what you need to do. You're going to work on whatever that big brain of yours gets curious about and you're going to make sure neither of your parents end up in jail. Or bail them out when they do."

She tried to laugh, God bless her. His heart clenched at his next thought and it took all his control not to curl his hands into fists while he said what he had to.

"You're going to find someone, Vetta. Someone who makes you laugh, who makes you think and he's going to make you happy."

She shook her head in quick, jerky movements.

"Yes, you will. He'll give you everything you've ever dreamed of. You just have to do him a little favor and not beat him up for seven years before telling him he has a chance with you." His joke fell flat because she sobbed, soft and tiny, but there nonetheless. He leaned to whisper in her ear, wanting her to be sure to hear him. "You deserve to be happy, Vetta. To have someone just for you, who'll be everything to you and you to him. Someday, I'm just going to be a fond memory. Someone who was lucky enough to have you in his life for a little while."

It sounded nice. Noble even. But it ate at him how true it was. Vetta would find someone else. He'd only be a memory to her, something she pulled out of her mind to think about when she'd be alone and reminiscing on her youth. While for him, she'd be the memory he pulled out of his heart every night and held close to himself as a testament to all that he'd given up in his quest.

"What about you? Are you going to find someone else in Montana?"

He could lie. He probably should, but there wasn't an answer that wouldn't hurt her. "No. I'm married to my work. That's the most important thing in my life. It has to stay that way."

"What if she understood that? What if she was okay with being second?"

His lungs refused to take in air. "Don't ask me that."

"But—"

"If I loved her, really loved her, she wouldn't be. I can't let that happen."

"What's so wrong with loving someone?"

He sighed. "Nothing. Loving someone is wonderful. It's beautiful, especially if they love you back. But it's not for me. I promised my mother I'd do everything I could to find a cure. I can't do that if someone wants as much of my time and attention as she'd have every right to expect. As much as I'd want to give her."

He felt when resignation took her. "Then it really is over, isn't it?"

She didn't need an answer, but he nodded anyway. She pulled back from him, removed her hands from his and sat ramrod straight in her chair, her face devoid of any emotion at all. He knew he'd lose her—knew he'd lose her tonight, even—but somehow, he'd expected it to be different. He wasn't prepared for her absolute withdrawal.

"If you'll excuse me, I require a moment in the ladies room." She rose, still graceful despite the stiffness in her limbs. He watched her leave, but no matter what might happen when she came back, Vetta St. Claire was already gone.

ଓ

Until they reached the front steps of their building, Vetta had never thought a person could bleed to death without ever spilling a drop.

For a few seconds in that restaurant, she'd been prepared to offer anything—anything—if he'd given the slightest inclination that they might have a chance together. It was so close to begging she almost threw up once she realized it. She'd spent far too long in that opulent bathroom, staring at a reflection she didn't recognize and wondering who she'd become.

Five weeks ago, she'd been a driven, self-empowered scientist on her way to proving...well, nothing important, but she'd at least had a firm grasp on what was important in life; family, security, personal challenge. And she'd had those things. It was enough for her. It *had* been, anyway.

But now she'd gotten greedy. Curious. Terrified. So terrified of losing something she'd never had. Of letting her only chance of ever feeling what Travis made her feel get away and so she'd grabbed on with both hands before she even knew what it was. But she knew now. She looked in her own eyes and knew she held love—pure and beautiful—in her hands. She couldn't have comprehended what it would cost her to let it go.

Or how much it might hurt to be let go of.

When she'd finally come out, Travis was waiting with the fries served and the champagne poured, oblivious to the life-changing understanding she'd come to. He watched her walk toward their table, his gaze feeling like he was memorizing as much of her as he could.

Let him, he's the one who's leaving, she'd thought, then contemned herself for it. He'd never offered her anything he hadn't given. He'd even warned her, not that she'd needed it. She'd been privy to too many of his relationships over the years. They never lasted and that's how he wanted it. It wasn't his fault she'd shoved them to a place they'd never meant to go. That she'd fallen in love with him.

So they ate. Politely, saying almost nothing. Twenty minutes later, she had no idea what passed her lips. She'd just wanted the night to end. To say goodbye, wish him luck and hope to escape with as much dignity as the other women who'd failed to keep him. She'd never thought to wish herself as wise as them, but here she was. What's more, she was in the strange position of respecting them.

They walked into the building and down the hall dividing their labs, side by side, her heels clicking on the concrete, not even their shadows touching in the harsh overhead fluorescent lights.

"Thank you for dinner," he mumbled, staring down at his feet.

Not that you ate much of it. "You're welcome." She took a deep breath and faced him. "I really do want the very best for you, Travis, no matter what...or who that might be. Take care of yourself...and thank you for—" God, how did you thank someone for changing your entire world?

"Vetta." He reached for her, but she couldn't let him touch her. If he did, she'd shatter. She'd beg. She'd do all the things she promised both of them she wouldn't. Instead, she backed away, putting her hands behind her back reflexively.

He stared at her. Sad and knowing. She wanted to hate

him for that, for understanding her so well and still letting her go. But all she felt was relief that he didn't need to break her to leave her. That he wasn't going to hate *her* for pushing him away. She'd get through the rest of her life if she didn't have to wake up in the middle of the night, knowing the man she loved hated her somewhere far away.

"Goodbye, Vetta," he said, softly, his hands in the pockets of his khakis. Forever, she'd remember the way he looked and sounded when he said it. Resigned, lost...sure.

She turned away, reaching into her purse for her lab key. She heard the *clinkle* of his, the rough insertion and twist of his lock and...a grunted thump. Frowning, she turned around and found Travis staring at his door. "What's wrong?"

He twisted to look back at her, confusion etched all over him. "My door won't open."

"Did you use the right key?"

For just a second, the familiar sarcasm surfaced, showing in the twist of his lips. "You wanna try?"

"I am generally better with complicated machinery." Her muscles relaxed as she crossed the width of the hall, her breath coming a little easier. This was a better way to say goodbye. As if it were any other day. She took the knob in her hand and twisted it easily. "See? No trouble at all."

"Try pushing, princess."

She did, but the door didn't so much as creak. With a frown, she tried again. Then it hit her. "Do you smell that?"

"Smell what?"

Vetta looked around the door, picking up the faint scent of...glue? Then she saw it. There, in the space between the doors, the dull shine of not-so-fresh, three-thousand lb., two-minute drying epoxy. She followed the trail and found herself circling the entirety of the threshold. Even the bottom had been sealed to the concrete. Obviously, no chances were being taken that anything less than a bulldozer was going to open that door.

Travis must have caught her line of sight because he pulled in a hard breath. “Is that what I think that is?”

“Only if you think it’s a glue-cemented door.”

“There’s only one person who’d even think of doing this. Tonight,” he added, because they both knew Vetta most likely had thought of it plenty of times. In fact, that was the purpose of purchasing the epoxy months ago.

She heard him come to the only conclusion possible at the same time she did. “Jade.”

Chapter Eleven

They said nothing as Vetta unlocked her own door, both of them well aware of what Jade was up to. The queen of machination wasn't letting them end it with a nice dinner and a kiss goodbye. Not that Travis got even that. Vetta was skittish again. He made sure not to touch her, but the charge coming off her was like a magnet. She wanted to be touched. She wanted to be held, to be loved. If she weren't fighting it herself, he wouldn't have had a chance against it.

"Why exactly does Jade do this kind of thing to you? Dumping you into situations and letting you wiggle your way out of them?" That part of their relationship had always confused him. Jade redefined the Mama Bear, prepared to club anyone to death who might threaten her chosen cub. And yet, that cub was often sent to the deepest waters of the river to see if she could float.

"You've never seen a mother bird shove her baby out of the nest to teach it to fly?" She led the way to her stairwell, never looking at him. The idea was for him to sleep on her couch until morning, when they could have a professional come look at the door. Of course, he had no idea what kind of professional covered the removal of a door, but Vetta no doubt had a man on retainer. With Jade around, one could never be too careful.

"Of course. Sucks when the baby doesn't figure it out in time, though."

"Jade has faith in me." She opened the door to the stairwell and gasped.

Curious, he looked over her shoulder, immediately seeing what had Vetta in stasis. His eyes followed the trail of white rose petals up the stairs and into the apartment where a warm golden glow emanated. "Looks to me like she's hedging her bets a little this time."

"What does she think she's proving?" Vetta muttered, less to him and probably not even to herself. She moved forward, letting him take the brunt of the door's weight, hitting the light and starting up the steps, her shoes pushing aside the pristine petals as she went.

Travis traveled slower, taking care to step in her footsteps so as not to crush another petal. Vetta might be able to ignore the sentimentality of them, but he couldn't. When he reached the top, it was pretty much what he expected to find. Lit oil candles colored the room from various surfaces. The mahogany dresser beneath the window alone had about eight. Small glass globes directed a path down the hallway, lit with floating white candles in the shapes of flowers. The middle of the runway had a repeating strip of hearts drawn with more petals.

Vetta stood, hands on her hips, glaring down at the romantic setting as if she could will it all to catch fire and burn until it disintegrated. "You realize she couldn't have done this alone," she said. "She probably got the lab techs to come up here and do this. They're young and stupid enough to buy any romantic crock she sold them." She tilted her head to the side. "Or she offered them a hundred bucks. For two, they'd probably hand-carve our initials into the walls."

"Probably not a good idea to look in your bedroom then."

She finally looked at him, her glare accusing. "You're happy about this."

"It's a sweet gesture from someone who cares about you. What's not to enjoy?"

"The fire hazard, for one. Who leaves candles burning unattended? And those petals are probably flammable."

Damn but she was cute when she was kicking up a fuss over absolutely nothing. "If you don't shut up right now, Vetta, I'm going to kiss you."

She cut off her diatribe, her mouth still open from her pause to take a breath. She let it out, her gaze searching his face for something. He didn't know what it was, but he hoped to God it was there to be found. He moved closer to her, relief filling him when she didn't automatically step back. She didn't flinch when he lifted his hand to touch her face, either.

Carefully, so carefully, he traced the curve of her cheek, then moved his hand into the masses of her hair to pull her flush against him. Her hands both lay on his chest, the last defense against what was between them.

"Tell me it means something to you," she said, her mouth less than an inch away, her eyes already closing for him. "Tell me *I* mean something, Travis. Give me that much."

He sighed. He wanted so much to take her mouth, to taste her one more time. If he could kiss her, he could drown out all of their pain, all of their pride and they could just be together again. For one more minute, everything would be all right again.

But it wouldn't be.

He pulled back from her, looking down at her. She stayed close to him, looking up with knowing eyes. She would have let him kiss her, let him make love to her even, but she'd known he wouldn't do it if it would hurt her.

"Why is it the only time you ever ask me for anything, you ask for my soul?"

Her hesitation was more than self-defense. He could see her searching for an answer that wouldn't hurt him, either. Didn't she know there wasn't one? "Because you're taking mine with you."

Apparently, she did. "Damn it, Vetta."

"I love you, Travis. I know you don't want it, but it's here and it's real. No matter where you go or who you become, I'm going to spend the rest of my life loving you. I know it. I need you to know it. You're leaving. I can't stop that. I only want to know that I didn't lose you for nothing. Please, I need to know—"

He kissed her then, his emotions too strong, choking him because he couldn't say them and he couldn't let her go on. She kissed him back, hungry, desperate, sobbing, but giving. Still giving...

It broke him, crushed him, to know what each caress was costing her. But still, she gave to him. He couldn't deny her, couldn't hold the words back if he tried. He didn't have it in him to lie to either one of them anymore.

"I love you, too," he whispered against her cheek. "I've been in love with you forever, Vetts. There's never been anyone but you and there never will be. Ever. Do you understand that? Will you remember that? *Ever.*"

She began to cry in earnest, holding him to her. He picked her up, pulling her long limbs around him before they fell to the floor and made love where they stood. It was only a few steps to the end of the hallway, to the open doorway of her room, where a sea of rose petals covered her bed. He only noticed them when they fell together, he above her, hearts fused and petals rising to flutter around them.

This was forever. Her and him. No matter what happened come daybreak, this was the moment he was born for. Loving Vetta. And being loved in return.

She pushed at his sports coat, leaving him to shrug it off while she worked at his shirt buttons. He didn't bother taking the shirt off, instead leaving it on so he could undo the tie at the back of her neck. The dress, its fine fabric relieved at no longer straining to stay with her, eased over her collarbones to reveal her breasts to his hands, to his mouth. She whimpered when he took her into his mouth, undulating beneath him like fire.

Her hands left their frantic search of his torso to work at the buckle on his belt. The clank of the pin sliding free led to a wisp of sound as she pulled the leather out from the loops and tossed it away. She wasted no time undoing the button and fly, reaching to find him and lead him toward her. With a groan, he gave himself over to her, the silken touch of her hand, the glide of her stroke. She opened herself to him, guiding him to her and crying out when he pushed deep inside with no further preliminaries.

He sank into her, into the wet vise of her flesh, into the welcome love of her embrace that he always tried to deny feeling before. He let it wash over him, closing his eyes and bowing his head to her breast. Warmth of a different kind seeped through him, taking all the pain of the night away and leaving only the sweetness of relief. Relief to be with her. "God, that never stops being amazing."

"I know," she said, half moan, half rough whisper. Her entire body quivered beneath his, waiting for him to move.

Travis raised his head again, meeting her passion-laden gaze with his own. His body ached to take her and lose all his regrets in her gasps and sighs, knowing that in this, at least, he could be everything she needed. But his heart, the one part of him he'd never allowed past the bedroom door—on purpose anyway—wanted just a second more. It wanted to remember the look on her face when he joined with her, from the misty moss color of her eyes to the sunset rose color of her cheeks to the way her mouth made that slight moue as he slid home. Hell, *he* wanted to remember. Always.

She lifted her hand, her fingertips catching his bottom lip. Curling upward, she brought her mouth to his, hungrily nipping and leading him back down to the mattress. She held him with her whole body, weaving a spell around him. It wasn't hard. He wanted to be taken under. Wanted to feel what it was to give everything and know she was giving just as much back to him.

They began moving together, clinging, speaking, breathing as one. He held her hips, she locked her arms around his neck and they lost themselves in sensation. His mouth traced the line of her throat. Her belly slid against his, wet with sweat and the heat growing between them. She moaned, rolling her hips against his forward thrust. When her back curved upward, he was surprised to feel her taking over. Soon, she was all but riding him from beneath, her tight nipples gliding along the wall of his chest and all he could do was stare down in wonder. She was the most beautiful thing he'd ever seen, the most amazing force he'd ever known and possibly more woman than he would ever deserve.

But she was his. Tonight, not even his doubts could take that way.

Taking one of her hands in each of his own, he pinned her in place, slowing the delicious torture she'd been putting him through. He ground his hips into hers, near growling himself when he lodged impossibly deeper. His mouth dropped to her neck, following the warm pulse there with a wet, sucking kiss.

Continuing the deep movement, he spread her thighs wider around him. When she was as boneless as he wanted her, the only sound between them the faint whimpers of her pleasure, he finally began to pull back. Her protest was short lived, if the intake of breath he felt against his lips could be called protest, because he surged back, harder than before. Over and over, he drove her into the mattress.

"Travis," she whispered, her voice close to a cry.

"I can't stop," he answered through his gritting teeth. His soul poured into each moment, the force and fire of his feelings almost more than he could bear.

"I don't want you to." She met his fervor, matching it until he was all but insensate. She clawed his shoulders just as she threw her head back and gave a keening cry, her body clamping tight around him in every way. Lost to all but his instinct, Travis wrapped his arms around her and let himself go, pouring into her while burying his face in the curve of her throat until the painful pleasure abated.

Afterward, he held her until she slept, drying her tears with rose petals. He never slept at all. He watched moonlight drift over her, memorized her every curve and hollow and told himself there had to be a way. But as the hours passed and night bled to day, he had yet to come up with one.

He stayed in the bed as long as he could, but his conscience got the better of him. Making love to her was a promise he wasn't sure he could keep. It meant agreeing to stay. Breaking every vow he'd ever made to himself. To his mother.

Could he do it?

He wasn't an "if only" kind of guy. If he were, he'd spend all his time wishing for things he couldn't change. Until now, that hadn't bothered him. He'd just picked up the pieces and started over. This time, something wasn't right. Was it that the pieces were too jagged to come back together? Or was he just tired of trying to make something of nothing? Was Vetta right? Was he giving up too easily? He didn't know anymore.

He slid out of her bed and dressed in the dark, slipping out as he had the first time, only there was no Jade to catch him at the door. Just a row of flickering or barely lit candle votives to guide him back down the hall. He padded across the wood floor in his socks, carrying his shoes with him down the stairs. Once there, he pushed his feet into the worn leather and let them take him out of the building to the cold misty March morning. He wasn't sure how long he walked, or even how far. The sun rose, seeping sunlight through the marine layer until even he noticed it.

All the answers he could think of involved someone giving up something that was too important to them. If he stayed, he'd have to turn himself into one of Vetta's leeches. If he left, he'd have to ask her to leave the lab, the only stable home she'd ever had. He couldn't see her abandoning her bastion of security any more than he was willing to abandon his.

He stopped walking, realization pouring over him like warm sunshine. Maybe there was a way they could both have what they wanted...if both of them were willing to take on a big risk.

He could stay, hell, he'd even let her fund his work...so long as she was willing to work on it with him. She couldn't help that she had money, no matter how he cringed at it. But it would be a major risk for her to take part in a study of actual importance. As big a risk as he was taking in trying again. But if she were willing to try, it could be their best solution.

Feeling suddenly more hopeful than he'd been in months, Travis trotted back to the lab, climbing the steps and entering the tiled foyer. He almost passed the mailboxes, but he stopped, figuring it'd be a pain to come back out and get any of it later. He'd already come to only checking it once a week since there was never anything in it. Maybe today was his lucky day.

He snorted his derision but pulled his keys from his pocket anyway. He opened the metal door and blinked at the large envelope waiting inside. If he didn't know better, he'd think that was an acceptance package. But it couldn't be.

With shaking hands, he reached for it, prying it out of the aluminum body of the mailbox and unfolding it with mounting disbelief. It wasn't possible. It just wasn't. Not from these people. Fingers growing more and more numb, he fumbled with the seal and finally reached into the envelope, finding the smallest article inside. A three-fold brochure, colorful and glossy, showed a white luxury liner on its front fold, all but smiling at him in betrayal. The lump in his throat disappeared as anger surged and heated his blood.

He'd been stupid to think he could trust her.

But all that was going to end now.

Vetta woke alone under the comforter, the scent of Travis still on her pillow. Her eyes ached, her head throbbed and yet, there was a bone-deep satisfaction in her.

Travis loved her.

It didn't change a single thing about their situation, but she felt light with hope anyway. She buried her face against the pillow, inhaling deeply, her mouth being tickled by an errant petal. There was only so long she could stay in the warm cocoon of her bed, so she made herself pull back the comforter and get up. Her robe hung from the back of her bedroom door, so it was only a few steps to reach for it. Travis had finished removing her clothes while she slept, hanging the crushed dress in the open side of the closet, lining her shoes beneath it neatly. She was still shaking her head at the gesture while she made her way down the hall, tying her robe sash.

The candles had all been extinguished—or had they just burned out?—leaving only the mess of petals on the floor. She had the sentimental urge to collect them all in a box and save them somehow. For what purpose, she didn't know, but it was obvious a few dozen roses had sacrificed themselves for her happiness. It was only fitting that she should preserve something of them.

She picked up a handful of the shell-shaped petals, carrying them carefully to her bookcase. She selected *Ansem's Astrological List of Coordinates*—basically a ten-thousand page directory of coordinates and correlating heavenly bodies—and hefted it to the dining room table. Nibbling on a banana from the fruit bowl, she placed petals in between the pages in clusters of five or so. Carefully, closing the book, she carried it back to the bookcase and pushed it into its tight fit. With any luck, the pressed petals would be dried in a few weeks. Then she could keep them next to her bed, to touch, to smell and remember.

She looked around, the stillness of the apartment finally registering. Wherever Travis went, he should have been back already, shouldn't he? It wasn't as if he could go to his apartment. Frowning, she went down the stairs, looking for him. She didn't have to go far. He was in the lab, sitting in Jade's chair, holding a manila envelope in his hands.

"Travis? What are you doing down here?" His stillness alone was a warning. She shivered, and not from the cold of the floor or the morning air. "Travis?"

"You slept so well. I've never seen you sleep so long," he said, his voice blank and his head still bowed to the envelope.

"I...I didn't realize. What time is it?" She looked around.

True, she didn't usually sleep like regular people, but she'd been emotionally wrung out. It wasn't exactly surprising.

"I couldn't sleep. I spent all night, trying to figure out how we could make everything work out. How we could be together. Because people in love should be together, right?" He wasn't being pensive. He was angry. So angry he wouldn't even look at her, but the line of his back was tight, almost pulsing with rage.

"I thought a walk might do me some good, so I went out. Thought I'd check yesterday's mail while I was at it, since I didn't get around to it in all the excitement."

"Travis—"

"I got an appointment from the Brassett Board. Three years of funding. They've offered me the brass ring, if you'll forgive the pun. Enough money to update my equipment. Hire a staff, if I want. They think I'm going places with my research. That my experience in the field is invaluable."

How he said it so dispassionately, she didn't know. Her heart jumped, leaped almost, in her relief for him. "That's great! It's fantastic—"

"It's bullshit!" he snapped, turning around finally, his jaws tight and his eyes so full of disdain she felt physically impacted by it. "It's not real and you know it."

The smile that had burst from her melted away, forgotten in an instant. "Know what? What are you talking about?"

"I didn't earn this. The Brassett Board decisions weren't to be announced for another couple of weeks. Suddenly this just shows up out of the blue? Enough money for me to do whatever the hell I feel like? Enough money for me to stay here with you. It's too fucking convenient."

Vetta gaped at him. "You think I had something to do with this?"

He sneered. "Of course you did, I'm not an idiot."

"That's certainly debatable at the moment. I can't make sense of a single thing you've said."

He stalked forward, taking hold of her arms and glaring at her. "You just had to do it, didn't you? I told you I was leaving and you up and called your father. Pulled strings. Did whatever you had to do to ensure I didn't go anywhere."

"You're a scientist, Travis. One with dedication and experience, if I remember correctly. Is it completely out of the realm of possibility that you *earned* that appointment?"

"Yes. It is. When thirty other applications get turned down in a year, you bet your ass it's not possible. Someone intervened and before you throw Jade under the bus, I have the mail keys. She couldn't have planted this and she doesn't have the pull to make this kind of grant happen. Your parents wouldn't know how. That only leaves you." His eyes blazed with betrayal. He let her go, as if he couldn't believe he'd touched her willingly. "All I asked from you was that you let me handle my problems on my own and you couldn't do it."

"I *didn't* do it!"

"Don't lie to me," he growled. "Not when I'm holding the letter in my goddamned hand!" He shoved the manila envelope into her hold. "Open it."

This couldn't be happening. All the obstacles were gone and yet, now they were falling apart. "No."

"There's nothing in there but the truth."

Her hands shook as she looked down at the large packet. She flipped open the flap and pulled out the three articles inside. One was a three-page letter, congratulating him on his acceptance and a brief outline of the grants and the details of the ceremony. The second was a formal invitation for him and a guest. The final was a white and gold embossed ticket—a yacht ticket. The Brassett Board of Trustees, cordially inviting him on the bay tour of the San Diego Harbor for those attending the award ceremony aboard the ship, *Solstråle.*

Her mouth went dry and all her dreams withered in an instant. So close...but so far away. The story of her life.

She put the three pieces back into the envelope and closed it securely. He watched her the whole time, waiting for her to say something he could pounce on, probably. Waiting for her to deny it, or even beg forgiveness. Instead, she handed it to him calmly.

"You're right. The truth is in there. It's just sad you're too blind to see it. Or maybe just too afraid."

"What?"

"I didn't rig your grant, Travis. I didn't have time. I was too busy trying to figure out how I was going to let you go with some degree of dignity. So, the only other option is that you actually earned it. But that can't be it, can it? Because you failed and you gave up. Because blaming me means you don't have to dig up the courage to try again. If that makes your life easier, go ahead. Blame me. As long as you realize you've just thrown away the two best opportunities you've ever had because you were too afraid to deal with them."

"Afraid? *You're* calling me afraid? You live in terror of being seen outside this damn fortress of a building, hiding in it and behind it. In all the time I've known you, all you've done is hide. Hide yourself, hide your potential, hide from the responsibilities of being gifted with a mind like yours. It's not the cameras and the fortune hunters you're afraid of. You're afraid of not measuring up to your parents. You think you'll never be as beautiful as your mother or as successful as your father's family, so you don't try at all. Don't talk at me about hiding until you come out of the cave yourself."

It hurt, oh how it hurt. Especially that he was right. About that much, at least. But that didn't make her wrong.

"So is this what we're going to do, Travis? Rip each other to shreds? Go for the jugular? Kill this relationship before it gets really scary? Okay, we can do that." Moving without allowing herself to second-guess her decision, she brushed past him to the phone on Jade's desk. A quick unsnapping of the phone line and she held the heavy, multi-buttoned contraption in one hand. Not caring whether he followed her or not, she threw open her lab door and stared at his half-glass, half-wood door.

And flung the phone right through it.

The shatter and crash was pretty satisfying, actually. So was the stunned look on his face as he stared at the damage. Not finished with him yet, she grabbed his shirt near his belly and pulled until he was out in the hall. She stomped back into her lab and glared at him one last time.

"Good luck in all your future endeavors, Dr. Carmichael. Assuming, of course, you ever get the balls to have any."

Then she slammed the door in his face.

Chapter Twelve

Twenty-eight hours. More than a whole day. And still no word from Travis. Not a single ring of the phone, not even his apologetic shadow on the door.

Jade showed up near evening, interestingly silent about the blatant hole in Travis's door. She didn't ask questions when Vetta didn't greet her while viciously entering subjects into the study. So intent on what she was doing, Vetta hadn't even bothered with dressing in layers. What was there to hide anymore anyway? Jade didn't ask any questions fifteen hours later, either, when the lab assistants came in at their regular times and found Vetta still hard at work, which was a relief.

That was the nice thing about work. You could throw yourself right into it. The whole world could fall away and you wouldn't know about it because you were working. The only downside was running *out* of work. Then there was nothing but an empty world, you and your thoughts.

That had happened two hours ago and Vetta was tired of it. She'd finished all but the final entries, had read some projects her father's CEO wanted approved and applied payment to some of her favorite programs. None of which were the Brassett Board, something that got her all fired up again.

So Travis hadn't called. Hadn't come to his senses—assuming he had any—and hadn't apologized for thinking so little of her. Fine. Let him leave. Let him go work on his hormones, she was certainly done with them. Conclusion to the great Carmichael Libido Experiment: Clearly, man cannot power his brain and his penis at the same time.

"Um, Dr. St. Claire?" One of the assistants had the audacity to interrupt Vetta's mental vent, something the girl obviously regretted when Vetta found herself turning to her with a near snarl escaping. The student held a fluttering paper in her hands. "We have the winner."

"Any chance it's Harden Beefy?" Vetta imagined ensuring Travis going for a year without sex. Perhaps she could even sneak into his apartment at night and toy with him in his sleep, just to mess him up...

"Um." The girl looked a little troubled at the smile that felt purely evil on Vetta's lips. "No, it's a man named Sigwald Vasquez-Anderson. He fit ninety-eight point seven percent of the criteria. The next nearest match was only ninety-five percent."

Vetta's dream of torturous revenge faded. It was probably for the best. Travis would have turned down the deal anyway. *He* didn't take money from women. Her temper flared up hot and high, but this time she worked to tamp it down before speaking to her assistant.

"Call him and arrange an appointment to meet as soon as he can get here."

"Yes, Dr. St. Claire." She turned and practically ran to her desk for the phone.

Vetta strode through the otherwise-empty lab to her apartment door, picking up in her mind right where she'd left off; lambasting Travis.

He thought she was such a control freak she would bully her father into some elaborate plan so she could buy herself a lover? Why was she surprised? The man was just as obsessed as every other man when it came to her money. He acted like having a few hundred million automatically made her evil.

Jerk.

She dropped onto her couch, not caring that she was slouching or that she'd probably broken a spring somewhere under all that fluff. Since she was rebelling, she put her feet up on the table. There, *now* she was happy.

"What you think you're doing?"

"Being happy," Vetta replied to the stern voice from the hallway.

Jade stood there in, of all things, a *navy*-colored mumu with bronze-colored fronds at the hem. "Yeah, you look it. You ready to talk about what happened now?"

"You say it like it's my fault."

"No, I'm sayin' it like a tired woman. You and that man should just buy teeter-totters, it'd be easier to tell who's comin' and goin'."

"I'm sure the broken glass gave you a clue who went where," Vetta grumbled. Then sighed. There was no point in not telling Jade. Odds were she'd already been over to Travis's and gotten it out of him anyway.

"He won a grant and thinks I set him up to get it. That I'd go back on my word and trick him so I could *pay* him to stay with me. Can you believe the nerve?"

Jade just blinked at her.

Vetta rolled her eyes. "Look who I'm talking to. Just tell me you didn't do this." No sooner were the words out of her mouth than she closed her eyes and waved her hands at Jade. "Never mind. Don't tell me. I don't want to start fighting with both of you at the same time."

Jade only shrugged, wiping her hands on her thighs as if she had no hope of understanding what was going on. It was a little too real to be believed.

"No, I need to know." Vetta squinted and leaned forward to inspect her more carefully. "*Did* you have anything to do with this?"

Jade's frown was pure consternation. "Baby, I don't even know what you're talking about."

"The Brassett Board Award. Travis was named and because the presentation gala is taking place on Penny's yacht, he's assuming I set it up."

"How dare he accuse you of that! You'd never have left any proof pointing at yourself."

"Exactly." While Jade's faith in her was nice, Vetta had to admit, her reasoning wasn't exactly becoming. She *wouldn't* have left an obvious trail like a ship named after her. But it wasn't very inspiring to know all three of them believed her capable of it.

"I guess you better find out how it happened then."

"Why should I? He's determined to think the worst of me. Let him."

Jade rustled her way over to sit on the couch with Vetta. "Yeah, 'cause that's worked real well over the years."

"No lectures. It's completely out of my hands. It always was."

"You gave loving him a good try, baby," Jade soothed, patting the side of Vetta's hair. Hair she'd braided so tight it hurt to blink because Travis preferred her hair free and flowing. "You can remember that when you get old like me. Old and alone. With nothing to call my own. Well, except for my pride. We'll always have that."

Vetta leaned her head on Jade's soft shoulder, hoping that twitch in her lower lip wasn't a wobble. Just because the futility of being angry and hurt and heartbroken was finally starting to settle on her was no reason to be emotional. Travis Carmichael wasn't about to make her cry again.

"This has nothing to do with my pride and everything to do with trust. He says he loves me, but he doesn't *trust* me. It's not prideful to want to be trusted."

"No, baby, it's not," Jade said softly. "It's just prideful not to cry when you need to."

The wobble couldn't be stopped now. The stinging in her eyes and nose started and the boulder in her throat grew a few sizes. Jade opened her arms and Vetta fell into them, hearing Jade's comforting sounds and feeling the gentle palms rubbing her back. She consoled herself, as the soft fabric of Jade's dress turned a moist black, that Travis hadn't made her cry.

Jade did.

Travis didn't like himself. He hadn't liked himself since Vetta slammed her door in his face and he'd let her. He regretted it, of course, but he'd spent the last three days telling himself how right he was to have done it.

It'd be a hell of a lot easier to go if he believed it.

He dumped another box on the stack down in the lab. He had yet to figure out how a guy with practically nothing could fill so many boxes of stuff he couldn't part with. Considering how badly he wanted to leave and get started in Montana, he found himself lingering over just about everything he packed, taking more and more time with each box. He'd even called Dr.

Donaldson to inform him that he'd be a few days later than expected. Almost as if he were dragging his heels or something.

Worse, he was downright depressed over how many things conjured up memories of Vetta. Memories of arguments, pranks, classes, her smile, her laugh, her innocence, her passion. All of which then reminded him of her pain. Pain he'd inflicted that he didn't have to. He'd panicked, was all. He wasn't even sure why. The Brassett Board appointment should have been the answer to his prayers. Instead, it sat ignored on his desk.

No, not ignored. He was too aware of it for it to be that. It sat there, silently haunting and accusing. Just like his conscience.

Vetta was right. He *was* afraid. Terrified. He'd given it everything he had before, desperate for his work to matter. To make up to his mother that he hadn't been able to do a damn thing for her while she was dying. All she'd worked for, all she'd sacrificed for him and in the end all he could do was hold her hand and cry.

Maybe the work *was* guilt-driven. He'd considered that before, but knowing that truth didn't make it any less important to finish. But despite even the strength of his guilt, his efforts, passion and dedication, he'd failed. It was like losing her all over again, only worse. Somehow, it was worse.

The prospect of starting again, picking up the pieces of his study and opening the door to eventual failure he wouldn't professionally recover from... He couldn't even swallow, just thinking about it. Yes, Vetta *was* right. But that didn't change how he felt.

Not even about her.

Travis sat on the edge of Vetta's bed in his lab and held his head in his hands. When had it all gotten so fucking confusing?

It wasn't that long ago he knew what he was doing with his life. Now every direction he took seemed like the wrong one. Go. Stay. Neither one was right.

He started to get up, sick of thinking the same problem through over and over again, when his foot brushed something hard just under the bed. Looking down, he realized it was Vetta's laptop. He reached for the brushed-steel machine, running his fingers over the fruit-shaped insignia on the top. He tapped it with his fingertips, his insatiable curiosity starting to pique.

She was always tapping away when she thought he was asleep. Sometimes, he'd drift off, content just to have her with him. He'd wondered what she was drumming away at. Something important, given the way she nibbled her lip while she did it. Sometimes he'd catch her daydreaming, lost somewhere in that big brain of hers. Was her computer a way to find out what it was she thought of night and day?

It probably was.

But he couldn't dip that low in the morality pool, even if she never knew about it.

What he could do was write her a letter. An apology. And when he was going, he could leave the laptop in the lab for her to find. Cowardly, maybe, but better than thieving.

Or so he thought.

Opening the computer's screen, it automatically lit up to her word program, a single line visible on the current page.

#861: Have checked online sources for facing positions to test theory.

Was it his fate to constantly be blindsided by this woman?

Miserable as he was, he had to laugh. Leave it to Vetta to take notes on their love life.

He should have opened up a new file and written his apology. He knew it. His mother would, at that moment, be slapping him upside the head for sticking his nose where it didn't belong. But his mother wasn't there. The devil on his shoulder, however, was.

What else had she noted about him?

He hesitated, finger above the upward-arrow button. She had over eight hundred notes to choose from. Did he really want to know what her analytical brain had thought of his aggressive sexual appetites? Would it be anything like his childhood report cards? *Travis has great potential, but is too distracted... A joy to have in class; needs improvement in attitude concerning homework.* Had she graded him? Did she still think his fetish for dirty talk was so kinky? How much research had she put into keeping him up all hours of the night? Had she been watching internet porn for tips?

That thought was both funny and arousing. Vetta watching porn probably meant Vetta doing things to herself while watching porn...

He shook himself out of that train wreck of a thought. It would lead to some depressing one-handed resolution that would only make him miss her more. But the cursor still blinked in electronic temptation.

What the hell. It wasn't like he had much else to do.

He hit the button and watched the text on the screen rise. Reading backward would probably give him a headache. And he was already going to be in trouble if she found out. Might as well be in trouble for a good cause. He dragged the document up to its first page.

As expected, there were some generalities. *Travis is stronger than I realized. Must utilize positions that maximize his power. Perhaps* cuissade... *Quite virile. After a week of nightly sexual sessions, Travis is still not only actively seeking sex, but is quite vigorous through multiple emissions... This is good. Very, very good.*

Did that count as an A?

He frowned as he hit the next few entries. *Virginity is a turn-off... He seems to think other men might avoid virgins, but cross-referencing with already-entered data for PM search is contradictory. Males seem to prefer younger women by their own data and women noted that most of them lost their virginity and either didn't see their date again or the relationship terminated shortly thereafter due to dissatisfaction. Travis is unique. Not advisable to tell him previous status unless interested in ending experiment.*

He frowned. What did she mean *experiment*? And she better not mean what she sounded like she meant with *previous status*.

Of course, being Vetta, he was sure she did.

Fuck. That's what he got for assuming. He'd thought she'd at least been with Rey, that asshole he'd hated with every inch of his being. Rey had been around for months, the smug piece of shit. And Vetta had been hurt when the guy showed his true colors, something that never happened usually. She involved her feelings about as often as he did, which was probably what had stuck in his craw about her relationship with the prick. She'd smiled at Rey. Had talked to him, their heads bowed together over notes and scopes, and all the while, Travis had known Rey was simply biding his time. He'd tried to warn her, but she'd thrown his concern back in his face. He couldn't blame her, not even then. Travis didn't like to think back to his own foul mood back in those days and he hadn't handled the conversation well. Shit, he hadn't handled anything with Vetta right in seven years. Back in those days, though, it was worse. He'd been inexplicably angry every time he saw them together and it showed. When it was over, he felt like a bastard for being happy when Rey was finally gone. He'd never let himself dwell on why. He'd avoided the whys with Vetta as long as he could.

Couldn't avoid them now.

He remembered the day she must have made her notes. The way her eyes had changed while they were talking, looking slightly to the left. He'd practically seen her flip the record switch on her brain. Didn't make him shut his mouth though. No, she'd had to use her tongue to do that. Of course not before he'd said he never wanted to be with a virgin. Waxed poetically stupid on why he'd avoided them. Proved he was an ass is what he'd done.

He continued to scan, knowing he couldn't change the past or apologize now. What her found were personal things about himself he hadn't expected, things that were unwittingly endearing about her. *I would have expected the simplicity of his life to be difficult to deal with, but there's something nice about simple. Refreshing...*

Refreshing, my ass, he thought with a snort.

He only has one bottle of soap in his shower; hair and body. I have four; shampoo, conditioner, exfoliant and soap. He uses a washcloth. On everything. Is this a male thing? Must find his soap at store. I want to remember it when he's gone.

Funny, considering he preferred the coconut soaps she used. Should he tell her he'd been using a multipurpose soap that served as shampoo, body soap and dish detergent to cut costs or just keep that *refreshing* tidbit to himself?

He kept reading, note after note on her thoughts about certain positions (*Inversion is enjoyable, but not worth the backache when Travis is far more efficient in other styles.*) and how she viewed him (*He has the strangest way of tying his shoes. I cannot see a way this works in the laws of physics to keep them on his feet.*) and even her views on his situation (*He turned me down again today. This is especially confusing. Have never met a man other than Travis who didn't want financial assistance. Either I haven't been meeting enough men or earlier conclusion is correct: Travis is unique. Must do more research. And keep trying with Travis. At least his projects deserve funding, unlike others, i.e. Carl.*). He didn't know who Carl was but it didn't sound like he'd made a very good impression on Vetta.

Then again, neither had Travis for nearly seven years. So he couldn't go around throwing stones. Much as he might want to.

I'm going to miss him so much. I wonder what it'll be like when he's gone. Will he be happy? Will he miss me? Will he go back to sleeping with lab monkeys?

He barked a laugh before he could stop himself. How she got to calling his occasional bed partners "lab monkeys", he'd never understood. Her scientific version of a buckle bunny, he supposed. She'd managed to pick a fight every time she caught him with one, though. Had she loved him even then? Had every moment they'd spent together been because they'd cared more than they should? It all ran together in his mind as just part of life with Vetta.

I don't want him to go.

Travis closed his eyes and sighed. He knew she didn't. He even knew she wasn't lying about not setting him up. His gut had finally overruled his knee-jerk reaction when she threw her phone through his door, but by then it was too late. By then, his common sense decided it was better for her if he let her throw him out. Better to let it end cold and clean. Better to forget his moronic compromise.

I hope he finds everything he's looking for. Even if it will never be me.

It would always be her.

She would just never know.

☙

"*You're* Sigwald Vasquez-Anderson?" Vetta tried to bury her surprise. It should have been easy. For three days now she'd been unable to feel anything at all. Nothing made her smile, nothing made her cry, not since she'd pulled out of Jade's arms and mentally shut everything down.

Until now.

She stared down at her clipboard, then farther down to Mr. Vasquez-Anderson.

He glared up mutinously. "You gotta problem with that?"

"No," she said, her unexpected astonishment fading. She tightened her grip on the clipboard, grateful for the numbness returning her equilibrium. She'd need it now. Mr. Vasquez-Anderson was the last thing she'd have expected when she thought of The Perfect Man. She expected tall, handsome...clean.

Against her will, she'd expected Harden Beefy.

Her equilibrium threatened to shift back under emotional water. Unbidden, a memory of Travis flashed in her mind's eye. His smile as he tipped her nose down with his index finger, the warmth of his laughter all around her.

The squeak of her subject's boots on the floor snapped her

back to the present. Thankfully. She pulled in a breath, resolved to see this through. One more cursory look over her subject, however, made her frown. This could *not* be the most perfect man in the study.

She flipped through his application. Sigwald was employed as President of the Dirty Dozen Motorcycle club and a member of MENSA. He apparently took his job seriously, because all five foot three of him was covered in mud-spattered black leather. Except for his chest, which was bare of fabric but matted with curling dark hair and who knew what else. In fact, closer inspection might reveal all that fur to be a pelt of some kind—possibly roadkill—that he thought would heighten his image as dangerous and filthy.

A wiry man, his flat muscles were covered with red-brown skin that looked like it had spent way too many years in the sun. It probably had. Another two or three and it might crack when he walked. Ironically, his black beard was trimmed neatly and his equally black hair was slicked back to his nape where it extended in a wind-beaten ponytail. He might not care too much for the mud he collected, but he obviously took pride in his facial hair.

He had yet to remove his sunglasses so she couldn't get too clear a look at his eyes, nor had he pulled the half-smoked cigar from between his teeth. Given the "No Smoking" sign at the entrance of her building, right next to the yellow, oversize "Hazardous Chemicals Within" sign, she considered that a neon sign of monumental stupidity. This couldn't be the right guy.

"So who do I have to screw to get my million?"

No, she had the right one.

Dubiously intelligent, virile—if you went for short, dark and scruffy—he looked like he'd experienced all a person could possibly survive and his employment required he be better traveled than her mother. Whether he had a sense of humor or could listen to women was up for debate, but Vetta figured it'd be a short one.

"We'll be over here, Mr. Vasquez-Anderson." She pointed to her conference table on one side of the lab, already set with multiple copies of the contract. Jade stood to one side of it, setting out a tray of morning muffins. "But you'll have to extinguish your cigar, first. I have no interest in witnessing a chemical fire."

He looked her over, his head moving mechanically as he weighed her jeans and plain white blouse much the way she'd weighed him and seemed to find her just as lacking. "For a hot babe, you're pretty uptight."

She nodded. "I'm also known to opt for litigation when people blow up my property. Put out the cigar."

He shrugged, unhinged his jaw and dug the dried tobacco stump from his miraculously still-white teeth, then extended it with a smile. Vetta eyed the moisture on one end and the hot embers on the other. The things one had to do for science. She reached into her pocket and pulled out a pair of small tongs, lifting the foul offering and depositing it in a nearby stainless steel sink. A brisk flush of water from the faucet and it was dealt with. By the time she turned around, Sigwald was already biting into a muffin and stuffing another into his inner vest pocket.

At least she didn't have to worry that he wasn't greedy.

She looked at Jade to get her opinion. Jade, however, was busy frowning at the rapid disappearance of her favorite muffin type and didn't catch the silent inquiry. Not that Vetta needed it any longer. No doubt about it, Jade didn't like him.

"I'm not signing anything until I've shared it with my lawyer," Sigwald announced, finally abandoning the muffins for the laid-out contracts in the middle of the table. He rolled one, unread, in his hands then pushed it into the back of his pants. Vetta made a note to request a fresh copy from his lawyer.

"So, tell me, pretty lady," he said, dropping into a chair and biting yet another muffin, having apparently decided now would be a good time to pour on the charm. "Whaddaya want with me?"

What *did* she want with him? He was going to be utterly useless to her experiment. No one would believe this man capable of netting regular sex in the first place. But somehow, some way, he'd managed to be what hundreds of women said they wanted most in a man.

Thank God she'd never dated much. No one could blame her for this mistake.

But until she was able to double-check her work—perhaps even consider that there was a flaw she'd missed in her program—she would still need his input. Just in case.

Reluctantly, she cleared her throat and dived into the explanation of the experiment. "It's simple, Mr. Vasquez-Anderson. All I want is your body."

Chapter Thirteen

Travis was actually managing to get something done when he heard the yelling. Frowning, he went to the gaping hole where his front door used to be at the same time that Vetta's lab door was flung open.

"You're sick, lady, you know that? You shouldn't even be allowed to molest lab rats!"

Travis stared at the man coming out of the lab in shock. *That* was Vetta's sex-test winner? A biker? An *ugly* biker? Travis couldn't decide which was crispier, the weather-beaten leather or the sun-cracked skin. Halfway down the hall, the man turned around to yell again.

"I wouldn't take part in this experiment if you paid me *two* million!" He reached one hand toward his back waistband and Travis felt an eruption of panic. Vetta had just stepped into the hall, unconcerned and blasé as usual when people were yelling at her. But a man like that, reaching in just that way could only be reaching for one thing, for one reason.

"No!" Finally, all those drills on speed and the art of destroying a man with a smartly lowered shoulder had meaning other than paying for his education. Hopping through the door, he moved in a burst of speed. The solid contact of flesh to flesh and the whoosh of air leaving the other man's lungs gave him a sense of satisfaction just before the splat of their bodies hitting the concrete sounded in his ears.

"Ohmigod! *Travis*, what are you doing?"

Travis barely registered Vetta's cry as he got to his knees above the crunchy man who was wheezing for oxygen, his arms splayed out.

"Mr. Vasquez-Anderson! Are you all right?"

Travis sucked in a deep breath of his own, his heart beating like a runaway train, looking up at where she bent in front of him to check on the man who'd been about to shoot her with...a roll of paper?

Travis blinked at the blue and white roll still caught in the man's hand. Hadn't he been reaching for a gun? Not that he could blame him, really. He'd certainly wished for armaments when arguing with Vetta, but...*uh-oh.*

"Mr. Vasquez—Sigwald? Is anything broken?"

Sigwald?

Vetta was kneeling next to him now, checking Leather Man for injuries just before reaching out and punching *him* in the arm with the speed of a diamondback. "What did you think you were doing, Travis? You could have killed him!" she hissed.

"I thought I was saving you—"

"From what? A virulent ink allergy?"

Sigwald began coughing, drawing their attention to him. A gasp or two later, the man was eyeing them from behind his now half-lensless sunglasses. "I'm suing."

Vetta turned an evil eye on Travis.

He shrugged at her. "It was a misunderstanding."

"I'll be sure to add that to your obituary. Now go away before you get us both into more trouble." She shoved his shoulder again and turned her back on him. She returned to nursing the guy on the floor.

Fortunately, Leather Man was too intent on escape to let her. Coughing and wheezing, he managed to get to his feet and wobble out the door. Which left them alone in the hall.

Almost alone.

Travis looked over his shoulder when he heard a chuckling that had apparently been going on for some time. Jade stood in the doorway to Vetta's lab, a smile two miles wide on her face and a muffin the size of a fist in her hand. Then she winked, blew him a kiss and closed the door.

Now they were alone.

He turned again to his hallmate. Vetta's glare blazed at him, red stained her cheeks and her lips were in a grim line. It was unlikely she'd missed the byplay. Maybe if he hurried, he could get Jade to come back.

"You just couldn't leave without wrecking my experiment, could you?" She clomped to her feet and stomped to her door. It'd be funny to watch if she wasn't finding something else to blame on him.

"*Me?* The guy was calling you names and walking out long before *I* came into it."

Vetta rattled the knob but didn't get anywhere. "Jade! Open this door! I mean it, let me in right now!"

There wasn't a reply. One more point for Jade. Travis shuddered to think what the score was each month between the two of *them.*

Growling with irritation, Vetta turned and headed for the roof. Travis let her get halfway up before following her. Inevitably, she slammed the door on his face once he got to the top. He wearily pushed it open and stepped out into the morning sun, weak as it was in late winter.

Vetta stood there, arms crossed, petulance in place on her

face. "I hate you."

"I know, I love you, too." He leaned back on the door. She wasn't going to give an inch. Man, it sucked that he was the one who had to bend on this issue. If only he weren't wrong. "I messed up the other day."

She waited for more, eyebrow raised, expression bland.

"I panicked, okay?" No, it didn't look like it was. He sighed and continued. "I'm sorry. I know you didn't arrange that grant."

"How? You called my father?"

"No. I haven't called anyone. I didn't have to."

Her mouth lost its pinched appearance. Her hands even slid to her sides, but she still stared warily at him. "Why?"

It was his turn to frown. "Why what?"

"Why didn't you need to call anyone? Didn't you need to make sure you didn't fall for my evil machinations?"

"Vetta—" He took a step forward but she took three steps back, her eyes closed tight, tears slipping over her cheeks anyway.

"I turned myself inside out for you, Carmichael. I did everything I could to live for the moment, to just enjoy what we had while we had it. I had a thousand opportunities to make you stay, but I didn't take a single one of them. Because you *asked* me not to. But you couldn't respect that. You couldn't *believe* that.

"I was going to let you go, damn it! Why didn't you let me? Why did you have to make it harder than it already was? And don't you dare blame Jade. She wasn't the one who made love to me. She didn't lie and say she loved me. *You* did."

Part of him wished Leather Man did have a gun, because it would have been easier to take a bullet for her than to hear her say that. "I didn't lie. I do love you."

"Not enough," she replied, finally looking at him, her heart in her eyes; that beautiful, wounded heart. "Not enough to trust me."

He walked up to her, putting both hands on either side of her face, making her meet his gaze when she would most likely turn away. Hurt spiked him at the feel of her tears slipping through his fingers. "*Too* much, Vetta. I love you too damn much to stay."

"That doesn't make any sense. Either you love me or you don't. Either you stay or you don't. Stop making it sound like one thing has anything to do with the other."

"They do." They had everything to do with each other.

"I don't understand you," she whispered, curling her fingers over his wrists, but not to pull his hands away. To hold on. Man, he was a waste because he could finally breathe again at that tiny sign of acceptance.

"Yes, you do. Better than anyone." How could he tell her? How could he begin to explain? "You said it yourself, I was scared. I'm still scared. Maybe I did earn that grant—God alone knows how—but I'm scared as hell of it. But not as afraid as I am of what might happen if I let myself try to be happy with you. I don't know what I'd do if I failed at that."

She looked at him like he was the idiot she'd always accused him of being.

Maybe he was.

He looked miserable. Almost as miserable as she felt.

"Why does it have to be over? Why couldn't we ju—"

"Because I'd never be able to function in Colorado," he interrupted, probably sensing an offer he could never accept.

She wasn't even sure what words were going to come out of her mouth. Desperation had her in its grip again, but she held it in, biting her lip to keep from saying something stupid. Something she might hate herself for one day.

Travis gave her the few seconds she needed to take a deep breath before he spoke again, his tone softened. "Knowing you were waiting for me to come back, wanting me to. Knowing I probably wouldn't. I wouldn't be able to do my job. It wouldn't be fair to you, to let you hope. And it's not like I could ask you to come with me."

"Why not?"

He gaped. "Do you think I don't know how you work, Vetta? Look at this place. If there's a bigger example of abandonment issues on the planet, I'd like to see it."

Bristling, she decided to ignore the truth in his accusation. "So you were being kind to me? Setting me free?" Hard walls that had crumbled at the ache in his eyes rebuilt quickly. "Aren't you generous?"

She pushed out of his arms, almost disappointed when he let her take a few steps away. She shoved the feeling away, concentrating on the anger that had brought her up here in the first place.

"I knew what I was doing when I got in bed with you. I made the choice to let myself love you, knowing you were going to leave. You had no right to decide all by yourself how I was going to live without you."

"I didn't make it for *you*," he interjected when she took a breath. "I made it for myself."

She kept quiet only because she could see him struggling to find the right words.

"If I stay, I'll be with you but you're asking me to risk everything on the chance that we could make it work. It'll be more than my career on the line, Vetta. It'll be you and me. My heart, my soul. Everything I have left that means anything. Could you take wondering where you rate in importance to me, because I guarantee being second won't make you happy. You've been second to everyone you've loved all your life, you'd want more from me and you'd be right to. And *I'd* be wondering if I'm doing the right thing putting my work second to my life.

"If that wasn't enough, I'd still be spending every day waiting for it all to disappear. What if I fail again? What if no one else ever believes I can offer something to the cause again? What if I'm not enough on my own?"

She stared at him, wanting to hate him, wanting to shake him until his teeth rattled and he understood. "Of course you are, you idiot. Do you really think you'd have made it so long, so far, if you weren't?"

His frown remained cemented in place. "What if I made it this long out of luck, like you're always saying?"

"Oh, God, don't tell me that you're finally listening to *me*," she laughed, pain mixing with her love for him. The poor, stupid man. He was almost as dumb as she was. "I was *wrong*, Travis. Couldn't you tell from Sigwald down there? Did he really strike you as The Perfect Man?"

His face screwed up in confusion. "There's no such thing as The *Perfect* Man."

"Tell me about it. The point is that after all these years of arguing about who was smarter, both of us were wrong. Me, especially."

She wanted to laugh, wanted to fall down and stomp her feet laughing. Instead, she might just fall in a heap and cry. She turned away, looking through blurry eyes at the rooftops across from them. "I had it all planned. The experiment that was finally going to mean something. It was going to explain *everything.*"

"Vetta, I don't know what you're talking about."

"It's simple. I thought if I could find the perfect man and prove that he'd choose the security that money gave him over sex, over something as unscientific as love, I'd prove that men aren't worth the space they take on the planet. That's what my experiment was about. To prove they're utter morons who are too greedy to see what love has to offer. What *I* have to offer."

"Vetta—" She felt his hand on her shoulder, soothing, warm and loving. She squeezed her eyes tight.

"You were right, what you said in the lab about me. I am afraid I won't measure up. I mean, my parents are insane, but they've never had any problems finding someone to care about them. Not me. No man I've known has ever wanted me. All they could ever see was the money I came with. A trust fund with a mouth. You have no idea how much it hurt, to feel so worthless. The truth is that I needed a way to prove it wasn't me. So I told myself there was something intrinsically wrong with *them* and I came up with this stupid experiment to find The Perfect Man and make him give up women for money."

Travis stared at her. As if he didn't see the truth that had been right in front of them. How could he? She never had.

"You were the cog that didn't fit. A man with integrity. The only one who never cared about my money. I took that for granted all these years. I wasn't even counting you in my study because if I did, I'd see that it was all just...*bullshit.*"

His eyebrows rose.

She scoffed at him. All this time and he still thought she was too innocent to use the right word when the situation called for it. "I could come up with any experiment I want and it still wouldn't explain you. I couldn't blame every man on the planet for my own shortcomings because you were there, being everything they're not. You were with me when you hated me. Protected me, even. I would have given you everything I never gave any other man who's tried to be part of my life and you wouldn't take it. So when you said you were leaving...I knew what I was losing." She finally met his gaze, taking in the haggard stubble on his jaw, the hollowed-out look in his eyes. She tried to smile, turning to bring her hand to his bristled cheek. "Everything."

He winced, so she pulled her hand back. He didn't want to be her everything.

She gasped when his hands slid over her own clasped ones instead, pulling them apart gently so he could hold them in his grasp individually.

"I need to feel safe, Vetta. Montana is the only way." He held tighter when she tried to yank free at that. "Do you think I *want* to go? That I *want* to leave you? Being with you is the best goddamned thing that's ever happened to me. This decision is killing me, dammit."

Vetta freed her hands. He was seriously going to do this. Tear them apart. Break both their hearts. And for what? A principle? "If it's killing you, then why are you making it? Why are you throwing us away?" She didn't care that she sobbed, that he saw her pain. How could she hide it?

"Because I can't have what I want. I'm not like you. I can't have it both ways. Not everyone can have their cake and eat it, too."

She shook her head angrily. "Don't you go making this some kind of class issue. It's not about money, it's about *fear*. You're afraid, Travis, and you keep pretending that I'm not. I have challenged everything about myself for you, faced everything that scared me to be with you. Do you think that was easy?"

"No, but—"

"Good, because it wasn't. It still isn't. But you won't do that for me. You say you love me. You say you wish thing were different but you won't *let* them be different. You won't stay. You won't let me come with you. At some point, you have to admit that you just don't want to make choices that have any impact on your future at all!"

Travis spun away from her with a roar of frustration, kicking at the gravel and sending dozens of pieces flying. "What would you do? If you were me, in *my* shoes, what would you be prepared to lose? 'Cause I'm bound to lose something, Vetta. That's the way it works in the real world.

"If I fail in Montana…it's just a job. It doesn't matter at fucking all. But if I fail here, I lose *everything*. I've done that once so, yes, I'm fucking scared. Is that what you wanted to hear? I'm *scared*. But you don't know what it's like to have nothing and no one. You have no idea how hard it is to pick up the pieces and keep going when there's no good reason why you should. You can't understand, Vetta, no matter how hard you use that big brain of yours. So just go back to your experiment where the answers are all black and white because that's the only place in the world you're going to find them that way."

She looked up at him, wanting to speak, to yell and throw things at him to make him see reason, but just then, it clicked. In her mind, the answers lined up, the mistakes fell away and clarity burned like a lightning bolt.

It was *him*.

While she'd been toiling over paperwork and computers, he'd been living her experiment right in front of her eyes. And he'd just shown her what was wrong with it: a simple matter of perspective. Women could want whatever they wanted from men and it would make no difference. Men looked at the world differently, had different definitions and expectations.

They answered questions differently.

She could have kicked herself. It was so obvious now. Then again, hindsight always was. Travis had been onto something when he'd answered the questionnaire with pictography. They might as well have been speaking a different language.

Men didn't think in terms of love or money. They thought in terms of security and risk. Minimizing risk means better survival. Survival depends on security. Physical, mental, emotional, all things came to this point for them and they, not seeing any reason to make it more complicated, judged accordingly.

Which brought her back to Travis. Here he stood, on the brink of decision. The security he needed...or risking it all on a chance to have everything he wanted most? But what was he going to choose? What kind of chance did she really stand?

None, she admitted to herself with a wince. Not if she couldn't reason with him in a language he would understand. Would accept.

Tread carefully, she reminded herself, pushing a breath out as softly as she could. Then she did her best.

"I can't tell you what's the best thing to do, all right?" she called from behind him, making him turn suspiciously. "You're right. I've never lost everything. I've never not had a home to come back to or been left *totally* alone. I *don't* know what that's like, but I will if you end this. Nothing I have and no one I know is going to be what you are in my life, Travis. And it's the same for you, I know it is. But you can't live your life based on what you could lose. You can hold onto everything with both hands and still lose it, no matter what. Look at my parents. Look at *us*. Loving each other isn't changing the facts or the decisions we make. You have to ask yourself, what are you going to gain?"

"It's not that simple."

"Trust never is. That's what it really comes down to. You'll have to trust that I love you as much as you love me, forever. Trust that I'm not ever going to walk away from the only person that challenges my mind *and* my heart. The only one who makes me tremble with a look and fall in love all over again every time he touches me. Trust that if we fall down, we fall together. That we'll get back up together, too. Because that's what you'll gain if you take that grant.

"If you go to Montana, what will you gain? Will you gain satisfaction from someone else's work? From being alone with your memories? Will you be warm thinking your mother wanted a lonely life for you? Will *that* give you the feeling you've satisfied her wishes for you?"

He didn't move, not even to contradict her.

"What will you *gain*, damn you?"

He just looked at her, the cold wind blowing in a sudden burst between them. She couldn't hear his thoughts or know his heart, not there on the precipice of his decision. His eyes told her nothing, only that he had listened and was thinking about what she said. She only hoped she could live with where she fell in the balances.

Travis turned away from Vetta, glaring at the buildings in the horizon as if they'd personally wronged him. They hadn't, of course. Vetta didn't even wrong him, not even as she threw questions he couldn't answer at him. He couldn't even blame fate. If anyone had fucked up, it was him.

He didn't want to go.

It was that simple. He did not want to leave. He should, though. He should be so grateful and relieved to not be the one shouldering the weight. He should be happy to leave all the scrimping and stress and sense of failure behind. But he wasn't.

Truth was, he didn't want to quit his own work. He didn't want to leave this place or this life. Most of all, he didn't want to leave Vetta. She wasn't the only one who didn't know how to move on alone. But he'd been too scared to trust her.

No, too afraid to trust himself.

Faith in Vetta had never been hard to come by. Even as rivals, he never doubted her promises or her dedication. If he stayed, she'd be by his side, no matter what happened. Failure or success, she'd be there. And it wouldn't be leeching to look forward to having her arms to go to when either situation reared its head. Common sense made him admit that. If anyone were going to need support in either case, it would probably be Vetta. She wasn't used to either. But she was willing to overcome her fears for him.

Couldn't he do the same for her?

Didn't he want to?

He felt his frown deepen as he finally noticed the skyline in front of him. A whole bunch of industrial buildings, beyond that the slatted roofs of older homes and finally, the blue-gray haze of the Pacific. His entire life, this city had been his home. But this place, this giant pile of concrete and the woman who owned it...this was where he belonged. She was still waiting, patiently even, though patience wasn't exactly her forte. For what? For him to get some kind of sign from Providence? Were the clouds supposed to part while angels sang and dropped a figurative anvil on his head? Was that what he was waiting for to give in to what he wanted most?

Courage.

Vetta was right when she said he didn't have any balls. Then again, it would take a big hairy pair to commit to a lifetime with a woman who challenged him every minute of every day. Who pushed him and supported him and loved him, flaws and all. It was, he admitted, the kind of happiness his mother would have wanted him to have. All she'd wanted for him was a future that had more than hard work with nothing to show for it. It was easy to forget that last part. His work would give him purpose, but Vetta would make him happy.

Hey, maybe angels dropped those anvils after all.

"You ever look out at the view on this place?" he called over his shoulder.

He smiled to himself as she struggled to limit her sputtering. "What?"

"The view." He gestured outward, waiting for her to explode, and tried to tamp down his grin. If she saw it, she'd kill him.

"You're not going to tell me you just spent the last twenty minutes staring at the *view*."

"No, I wouldn't do that to you."

"Yes you would," she grumbled, but he heard her walking toward him, mumbling as her shoes scraped the gravel. "Lucky I don't push you off."

"It might ruin your chances of earning my trust," he agreed, turning toward her when she stood shoulder to shoulder with him.

"Was that what I was doing? Because it felt a lot more like hanging on by a thread."

Travis shook his head. "More like a good fishing wire." When she gave him a look that told him she might show him exactly what he could do with his wire, he smiled. "I was just thinking that I don't pay enough attention to the view around here."

He watched her nose scrunch in his peripheral vision. She

had no idea what he was getting at.

"I'm thinking I should pay more attention from now on." He peeked down after a few seconds of silence to find her glaring at him. Her arm snaked out and jabbed him in the shoulder hard enough to rock him toward the edge of the building. He laughed, earning more of her ire.

"You ass."

"What?" But he knew.

"I'm standing here, heart on my sleeve, for twenty minutes and you're going on about the view."

Travis roped an arm around her shoulders to pull her close, but she pushed against his chest, just to be difficult. He could tell by the relieved smile tugging at the corners of her lips.

"No, *I could never leave you, Vetta.* Or, *I love you, Vetta.* Not even a basic *Thanks for waiting so long.* Stop kissing my neck, I'm making a serious point—"

He took her mouth instead, shutting her up and celebrating at the same time. She clamped her hands around his biceps, kissing him back for all she was worth. When he finally let her go, she was too breathless to say anything. So was he, but she deserved the words. And he wanted to give them to her.

"I do love you, Vetta. And I can't leave you."

"Damn straight," she replied, nestling into his arms. "Jade would have found a way to smuggle me into your luggage somehow."

He laughed with her, glad neither of them would have to find out exactly how her nanny would pull off the feat. "We're going to drive each other stark raving nuts. You sure you're prepared for that?"

She nodded, pulling away far enough to look him in the

eye. There wasn't an ounce of doubt on her face. "The only thing I'm not prepared for is not being with you."

The tightness in his chest let go. This was the right choice. It might not be the easy one, but it was the one he was meant for. He cupped her face in both his hands, wanting her to be just as sure as he was. "You'll never have to find out what it's like."

"Promise?" Because she knew he wouldn't promise what he couldn't do.

He nodded. "Never."

She reached for him, her kiss a little wild with relief. With predictable results. Before long, the taste of her mouth wasn't enough. He wanted all of her. Wanted to brand her and know she was his in every way possible. He slipped her coat off her shoulders, surprised to find only a single T-shirt between his hands and her skin. He didn't think too hard on it, his fingers finding the front clasp of her bra in record time so he could push that out of the way as well. She sighed as deep as he did when he found her nipples to toy with.

He dipped down, sucking her nipple and abrading it with his teeth. She moaned, deep and throaty, just the way he loved to hear it. He could spend all day listening to that sound, but he was wrapped up in a kind of urgency. An urgency he wanted her to feel as fast and hot in her blood as it was in his. She laughed as his fingers undid the snap at the top of her jeans, eagerly pulling the waistband to lower them. He stopped when the denim was bunched at her knees, dropping to his own to kiss her through the silk of her panties. He ran his tongue over her, on top of the fabric, just enough to have her pushing back against him. Her fingers tangled in his hair, pulling tight. When he knew she was starting to get somewhere, he backed up and stood.

“Wh—”

“I have an idea.” He had about thirty of them. And that was just for tonight.

Rather than let her argue—because this was Vetta and that was what she did best—he bent, slipping a hand beneath her knees and sweeping her up into his arms.

“Uh, Travis,” she murmured, her eyes widening as she watched the door to the shed come inexorably closer. “Where are we going?”

He smiled down at her, wishing he had a hand free to spank her nearly bare bottom. “Worried?”

“Now that you mention it.” She squeaked when he hitched her a little higher in his arms with a chuckle.

“Don’t. Just had to get off the gravel. That shit hurts like a bitch.” He stopped in front of the door, setting her down on her feet before it. Then he took each of her hands, placing them flat against the metal door to brace her. A second later, he took hold of her hips, scooting her backward so that she bent forward.

Vetta looked over her shoulder at him, her braid slipping down, eyes narrowed while she tried to keep from laughing. “This is starting to look vaguely familiar, Picasso.”

Travis only winked. Then he leaned forward over her, taking hold of her braid and wrapping the end of it around his hand. He used the other to run over her flank. First, he cupped her breast, rolling her nipple until she sighed. Then he let it wander, down her ribs, across her belly, over her hip then to grasp her ass and pull her open before easing past her panties to find her clit. He loved that thing almost as much as she did, toying with it, using his palm to move her folds beneath the fabric, stimulating her with her own flesh.

It was a damn shame he had to take even one hand off her

to shift his jeans out of the way of his now-aching cock. He did it as fast as he could, interested only in being with her. He dipped a finger between the fabric of her underwear and her skin, pulling it free to slide out of his way. Now she was bared, glistening for him.

He didn't make her wait.

Hot, wet, slow. His only thoughts as he glided into her body, as if he were coming home. A gentle tug on her braid had her back arching, pushing her hips tighter to his. He pulled out as slowly as he'd gone in, pulsing and grinding against her to greater depths. "Travis," she breathed, his third thrust finally granting her some speed, some pressure. Some relief, but not enough.

"You like it this way?" He gave another slow grind before driving in staccato beats. "Or is this better?"

"Travis." It was a moan this time. He increased the pressure on her braid, arching her further, lifting her hips so that her clit would feel the teasing brush of his balls as he pushed into her.

"It'll always be like this," he promised, picking up speed with each plunge. The thickness of him rubbed against every part of her pussy, which tightened around him with small spasms. It was all he could do not to give in to them, but he wanted her with him for the whole ride. She tried to widen her stance, to push back farther, faster, but her jeans around her knees kept her legs tight together, making her cup him harder.

"Oh, God, Travis!" she cried now, as his hand slithered over her hip, between her thighs, purposely stroking her clit in tandem to his strokes. He all but covered her now, his chest to her back, his thighs on the outside of hers, and still, he kept up the deep onslaught.

"Don't stop, please... Want it...to last...forever."

“It will last, Vetts,” Travis whispered, his voice so gruff it wasn’t much more than a growl. “No matter what, we’ll always be together. I promise.”

That was the last thing he said, because they both turned frenetic once they were uttered. His hard, fast thrusts pushed her forward while his hold on her hair pulled her back, her own movements rocking them wildly while his fingers plucked her clit. The head of his cock fit right against that groove inside her and suddenly, she was there. Crying out, a scream of pleasure so intense he barely heard his own shout while he splashed inside her.

They stayed locked together, panting, for a long time, Travis once again running his hands over her back, this time soothingly.

She looked over her shoulder at him, gray-green eyes dark like smoke, cheeks flush with color, her pink lips puffy and parted. She looked satisfied and hungry, all at the same time. He smiled back at her, breathless.

“Tell you what,” she offered flippantly, blowing her bangs out of her face. “You can look at that view as much as you want.”

He laughed. Just like that, he knew he was never going to doubt this decision. Being with Vetta was where he belonged. More importantly, it was the life he wanted.

No, it was the life he was choosing.

Epilogue

"See, I told her the doves were a good idea," Svetlana Swinton said while studying a heavy volume of photographer's proofs. The giant black book was only one of three and this was the fourth time Travis knew of that she'd gone through them. Of course, he and Vetta had only been back from their honeymoon in Yosemite for two days. There was no telling how many times she'd gone through them while they were gone.

At least now he knew it wasn't a symptom of inexplicable panic that had him seeing stars and bright lights throughout the ceremony and wedding reception. Thanks to the army of photographers that Svetlana had hired, there couldn't be more than three complete seconds of the entire day not captured on film. Svetlana's current husband claimed to be a movie director and was slaving away editing most of the video as his gift. Vetta rolled her eyes whenever Svetlana mentioned it.

"That limo driver wouldn't agree with you," Penny St. Claire said, crossing the expanse of space where Travis used to play makeshift racquetball to sit on a couch next to his ex-wife. They made an odd pair, the mid-height, mid-built, martini-swilling billionaire—Vetta had broken the news about the family holdings in a hot springs, smart girl that she was—and the blonde flake dressed down in a loose cashmere sweater and custom-cut silk pants. It was hard to imagine them married.

Then again, when they were yammering on about who did what at a party, laughing themselves silly, it was hard to understand why they ever divorced.

Travis stayed quiet, listening with half an ear to the hum of conversations going on around him. Svetlana's soft, flirting laughter, Vetta's simmering argument with Jade over various fabric swatches and the value of curtains. It still boggled his mind how much his life had changed in six months.

Accepting the Brassett Board award was only the beginning. Despite the fun of watching Vetta hand out packets of Dramamine and listening to the ones for which it was too late, the two-hour ceremony and tour of the bay was romantic and meaningful. He couldn't lie and say he wasn't still somewhat rattled when he accepted the certificate and honorary check. But it wasn't too hard to drown out the fear when all of the St. Claire family was cheering at the top of their lungs. If he were honest, having so many people on his side at the most terrifying moment of his life was what brought the sting of tears to his eyes, but he didn't say as much to the chairman who patted him on the shoulder proudly for the photographers.

The next big surprise was Svetlana offering to plan their wedding, which meant consistent contact for several weeks. It was how Travis finally figured out how she could railroad Vetta so easily. Svetlana Swinton, when she wanted something, was a force of nature; much easier to deal with when one let her have her way and only came out for the aftermath. If Vetta ever had an interest in arguing, it would have been utter war. Thankfully, she was relieved not to have to think about the details of a wedding. She found it far more interesting to puzzle out the best way to convert his lab into a home. It only took a month for the two women to plan a wedding and learn the basics of architecture. The wedding went off without a hitch, with the small exception of those doves and their overflowing bowels on Svetlana's car. The rebuilding of his lab, however, was still a burr in Vetta's side.

The structuring of rooms according to what both of them wanted and the insertion of windows had been the easy part. Decorating them was driving her insane.

Or maybe it was just Jade.

Vetta had a set schedule with the contractor to build according to her plans. While he and Vetta went up to Montana to visit with Dr. Donaldson before starting on their delayed honeymoon, the contractor's crew was to turn his barnlike area into something more *house*like. Jade had stayed to oversee the changeover of Vetta's lab into Travis's base of operations—equipment delivery and installation, etc. At least, that's what they told her, and in that respect, the change in layout had gone smoothly. She'd even found possible candidates for his assistants. He and Vetta just hadn't gotten any of them to admit which of them helped Jade take the room they'd intended as a personal library and convert it into a nursery.

Since there was no getting Jade to admit she'd done anything wrong, Vetta was just trying to make the rest of the house theirs. Unfortunately, Jade insisted on helping...

"I'm not saying you didn't do a fantastic job, Svetlana," Penny said, disturbing Travis's speculation about his luck in having avoided being involved. "But their first wedding was nicer."

"There *was* no first wedding!" she said, a hint of her Russo-Nordic accent sharpening her tone. "How many times do I tell you?"

"Jade, I'm not making the kitchen sapphire blue and that's the end of it."

"Why, you don't cook anyway. And if you use that yechy color in here it'll throw off the colors in the nursery."

Vetta vibrated a few seconds, the energy coming off her enough to make her hair seem to stand on end. Closer to him, his new in-laws appeared to be building steam of their own.

"So help me, Penny, if you don't give up on this wedding that didn't happen I'm going to marry you again and make you wish you'd never heard the word wedding!"

Then, as if everyone but him had gotten some kind of memo he'd missed, all heads turned to him with a chorus of "Travis!" and a variety of requests concerning reason, sense and veracity, all on top of each other.

His first instinct was to shake his head and wiggle out of the St. Claire insanity as quickly as possible. But almost as quickly as the thought formed, he dismissed it. For years, these wacky people had been as close to a family as he ever had, steady in their affection and kindness. Steadier in their peculiarities, but they didn't have a lot of choice about that. If all they asked from him was to be the occasional voice of reason, he saw no rationale to disappoint them.

He rose out of his chair, stretching a bit while Penny and Svetlana waited patiently on the pillowy couch that used to be in Vetta's apartment. Vetta and Jade waited in the open kitchen, one on each side of the breakfast bar with arms crossed and frowns in place.

"Sorry, Penny, this really is our first wedding."

"See!" Svetlana cried with an elbow to Penny's shoulder.

He barely noticed, frowning. "Then who got married in the Bahamas?"

"That was *us*!" his ex-wife sighed.

"Oh! No wonder I remember the honeymoon..."

More than willing to leave his befuddled father-in-law to sort out what few marbles he had, Travis crossed to the kitchen and considered the two women waiting there the way he would any other pair of claymores.

"If I agree with Jade, she might not find a way to disable the birth control," he said, trying hard not to smile despite his wife's narrowed gray-green eyes.

"If you don't agree with *me*," she countered, as she always had and he hoped to God always would, licking her lips and sidling up to him. "You won't need the birth control. *Ever.*"

Well, that pretty much sealed the deal. "Sorry, Jade, sometimes, you gotta lose if you're gonna win."

Vetta smiled up at him, a bright, true smile that had nothing to do with flirting, and everything to do with love despite the healthy grumbling and pot clanging going on behind her. "It turned out pretty good in the end, didn't it?"

"Who said this was the end?" he asked, leaning down to kiss her, thinking of how much of their lives still lay ahead of them.

She laughed against his lips. "Not me," she giggled. "Definitely not me."

About the Author

Dee Tenorio is a sick woman. Really sick. She enjoys tormenting herself by writing romantic comedies (preferably with sexy, grumpy heroes and smart-mouthed heroines) and sizzling, steamy romances of various genres spanning dramas with the occasional drop of suspense all the way to romanticas. But why does that make her sick?

Because she truly seems to enjoy it.

And she has every intention of keeping at it!

To learn more about *Dee Tenorio*, please visit www.deetenorio.com or her blog, www.deetenorio.com/blog for details on her newest releases!

He's never lost a bet in his life but she's playing for keeps!

Betting Hearts

© 2006 Dee Tenorio

Cassandra Bishop's boyfriend is back. Only problem is...she doesn't want anything to do with him. Or his new fiancée. What the confirmed tomboy would like is to wring his neck. She might have done it, too, if he hadn't filled her in on the embarrassing truth that he'd left her at the altar because she wasn't woman enough to satisfy him. Her pride nearly settled for punching him in the nose...until she thought of something better—proving him wrong.

High on Burke Hallifax's list of cataclysmic nightmares is having to look at his best friend as a real female. But when her ex-fiancé makes his wedding a personal vendetta against Cass, Burke has no choice but to bet everything on her ability to out hot-girl the competition. Unfortunately, the entire town is betting as well—on whether Burke and Cass can pull off the makeover of the century...without losing their hearts in the process.

Available now in ebook and print from Samhain Publishing.

Printed in the United States
131764LV00001B/93/P

9 781599 989655